Victoria Torres, Unfortunately Average
is published by Stone Arch Books,
A Capstone Imprint
1710 Roe Crest Drive
North Mankato, Minnesota 56003
www.capstoneyoungreaders.com

Library of Congress Cataloging-in-Publication Data
Bowe, Julie, 1962– author.
  Birthday glamour! / by Julie Bowe.
      pages cm. — (Victoria Torres, unfortunately average)
  Summary: Victoria Torres has always had a family birthday party that she shares with her
beloved grandmother, but this year she is so impressed by her classmate's birthday party
at GlamaRama, the mall's newest spa store, that she decides that she wants to celebrate
her twelfth birthday there — and her mother refuses to do both.
  ISBN 978-1-4965-0533-0 (library binding)
  ISBN 978-1-4965-0537-8 (paperback)
  ISBN 978-1-4965-2358-7 (eBook pdf)
1. Birthday parties—Juvenile fiction. 2. Hispanic American families—Juvenile fiction.
3. Middle-born children—Juvenile fiction. 4. Mothers and daughters—Juvenile fiction.
[1. Birthdays—Fiction. 2. Parties—Fiction. 3. Family life—Fiction. 4. Mothers and
daughters—Fiction. 5. Middle-born children—Fiction. 6. Hispanic Americans—
Fiction.] I. Title.
  PZ7.B671943Bi 2015
  813.6—dc23
  [Fic]   2015003976

Designer: Veronica Scott
Image credits: Capstone Studio
Design elements: Shutterstock

Special thanks to the team of tweens who provided helpful feedback
on covers and design.

Printed in the United States of America in Stevens Point, Wisconsin.
032015 008824WZF15

BIRTHDAY GLAMOUR!

by Julie Bowe

STONE ARCH BOOKS
a capstone imprint

All About Me

Hi, I'm Victoria Torres — Vicka for short. Not that I am short. Or tall. I'm right in the middle, otherwise known as "average height for my age." I'm almost twelve years old and just started sixth grade at Middleton Middle School. My older sister, Sofia, is an eighth grader. My little brother, Lucas, is in kindergarten, so that puts me in the middle of my family too:

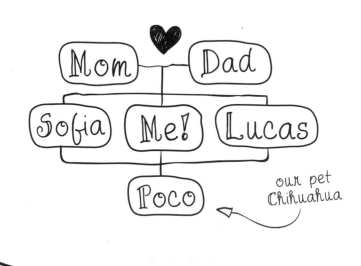

Mom ♥ Dad

Sofia — Me! — Lucas

Poco ← our pet Chihuahua

I'm average in other ways too. I live in a middle-sized house at the center of an average town. I get Bs for grades, sit in the middle of the flute section in band, and can hit a baseball only as far as the short stop. And even though she would say I'm "above average," I'm not always the BEST best friend to my BFF, Bea.

Still, my parents did name me Victoria — as in victory? They had high hopes for me right from the start! This year, I am determined to be better than average in every way!

Me!

Chapter 1

Party Fever

"Does Annelise have pierced ears?" Mom asks as we browse the This-N-That store at the mall. "Here's a pretty pair of earrings. On sale too. Three ninety-nine." Mom takes a pair of earrings from a display rack and shows them to me. Little teardrop-shaped diamonds dangling from silver wires. The diamonds sparkle so much under the shop's bright lights, at first glance they look real. Annelise is a girl in my class. I'm shopping for her birthday party on Saturday.

"She does have pierced ears," I reply. "And she loves glittery jewelry."

"Here's a bracelet to match," Mom says, taking a

thin silver chain from a hook on the rack. Little rhinestones dot the chain. "You could put the earrings and bracelet in a gift bag, along with some candy, and you'll be ready for the party."

I smile, taking the bracelet from Mom. My first middle-school party! When I started sixth grade a few weeks ago, I was worried it might be a *below-average* year. I didn't make the cheerleading squad. I was swamped with homework. And the locker my BFF Bea and I share gobbled up my books and wouldn't give them back.

But then I was chosen to be the school's mascot for football games, which is a lot of fun. I started studying harder for my classes. My locker is still a book-eating monster, but Bea and I are learning the trick to opening it (three turns of the lock and one swift kick).

And now, the first girl in our class is turning twelve. Annelise can be mean and bossy, so we are not best friends. In fact, we used to be *worst* enemies.

But things have gotten better between us lately. She's celebrating her birthday at the new GlamaRama! Beauty Boutique here, at the mall. It opened a few days ago.

At the party, we will get to put on makeup, have our hair done, dress up in glitzy costumes, and have our picture taken in a photo studio — just like we are real glamour queens! All my friends are invited too — Bea, Jenny, Grace, and Katie. We can't wait to get glammed up! I am *so* going to shine!

Annelise thinks it's a big deal that she will have one of the first parties at the new GlamaRama! store. But her parties are *always* big — last year her parents even rented a limo for all of us to ride around in!

My birthday parties are big too, but not in the same way. They're a big deal because my grandmother, Abuela, and I share the same birth date, so we always celebrate together with all our relatives. Sometimes the party is at my Aunt Selene and Uncle Julio's house on the other side of town. This year,

Mom and Dad are hosting! All my aunts, uncles, and cousins are sure to come. It's only two weeks away!

"Would you like a gift bag?" the sales clerk asks when I pay for the jewelry at the checkout counter. "They're free."

"Okay," I say. "Do you have one that says, 'Happy Birthday'?"

The sales clerk looks through a basket of gift bags. She takes out a bright red bag with balloons printed on it. "Will this do?"

I nod, even though the balloons look a little baby-ish. As she wraps the jewelry in tissue paper, I look around. I love this store, because you can buy lots of different things here. Everything from posters to jewelry to lava lamps. They even sell hermit crabs! My little brother, Lucas, has his nose pressed against a big glass aquarium, where lots of little crabs live. We have a family pet — our Chihuahua, Poco — but Lucas has been begging for a pet of his own lately. Mom and Dad keep telling him he's too little. *Un*fortunately, this makes Lucas very upset. He's only in kindergarten, so he still throws tantrums when he doesn't get his way. It's totally embarrassing when it happens in public!

"That one, Mom!" Lucas shouts, pointing excitedly through the clear glass side of the brightly lit aquarium. A little hermit crab scurries by, wearing a plastic football helmet on it's back. Hermit crabs don't have shells of their own, so they borrow whatever is handy to hide under. "Isn't he cute?" Lucas smiles sweetly. "*Pleeeease*, Mom? Can I have him?"

Uh-oh. Mom doesn't like it when Lucas begs for things at the store.

Mom walks over to my little brother and places her hand gently on his shoulder. "We've talked about this, Lucas," she says. "Dad and I don't think you're ready for your own pet."

Mom's right. Lucas can barely take care of his toys. Just last week he dented his scooter, de-trunked a plastic elephant, and lost five marbles in the sandbox. When it's his turn to feed Poco, he usually forgets.

My sister, Sofia, and I have to double-check to make sure Poco's dish has food and water when Lucas is on doggie duty.

Tears spring to Lucas's eyes. He squirms out from under Mom's hand and stomps his foot. "No fair!" he says, his voice sounding as thin and strained as a stretched balloon. "No fair, no fair, *no fair!*"

¡Uf! Here we go. Tantrum time!

"Lucas," Mom says, gently, but firmly. "Remember our deal? If you are good, we'll stop for ice cream on the way home."

A tear rolls down Lucas's cheek. His bottom lip quivers. I cringe, dreading the moment he morphs into the Tazmanian Devil, screaming and thrashing.

"We can visit the hermit crabs again soon," Mom adds, trying to avoid a total meltdown.

I step in. "And we can go to the library to get some books about them. That way, we can learn lots of facts about crabs before you get one."

Lucas wipes his cheeks with his shirt sleeve and

looks into the aquarium again. "You promise we can visit them? And get some books?"

"We promise," Mom and I say, together.

Lucas takes a big, quivery breath. "Okay." He taps on the aquarium. "I'll be back soon," he tells the crabs.

Mom and I exchange relieved glances. *Whew!*

I grab my gift bag, and we start steering Lucas toward the store entrance before he gets crabby again. But as we do, something catches my eye.

A row of brightly colored piñatas hang from the ceiling, all different shapes and sizes — a dinosaur, soccer ball, butterfly, and rainbow . . . there's even one shaped like a queen's tiara! I gasp. "Look, Mom! Piñatas!"

I rush over to the display. My birthday is coming up soon! We always get a piñata for my party.

"I've never seen one shaped like a tiara before," I tell Mom as she and Lucas walk up behind me. More piñatas sit on a shelf below the display. I hand my gift bag to Mom and reach for a piñata that's identical to the hanging tiara. It's covered with glittery pink and silver tissue paper.

"What a pretty crown," Mom says.

"*Tiara*, Mom," I correct her, holding the piñata over my head and striking a queenly pose. "That's more glamorous than a *crown*."

Mom laughs and does a royal bow. "My apologies to the *queen*," she jokes.

"The dinosaur is better," Lucas says, pointing to the bright green T-rex hanging from the ceiling. "Can I get one, Mom?" Lucas jumps up and down, reaching for a dinosaur piñata. Fortunately, he's too short to touch them.

"Your birthday was this summer, silly," I tell Lucas. "Now it's *my* turn for a piñata." I hold the tiara out to Mom. "*¿Por favor?*" I ask. "*Pleeease?* For my party?"

Lucas stops jumping. His mouth drops open, and his eyes go as buggy as Poco's. "If *Vicka* gets a piñata, then *I* get a hermit crab!"

He pinches up his face and stomps his feet so hard

the glass figurines on a nearby shelf clink against each other.

The sales clerk looks over.

"Stop it, Lucas," I snap. "You're an *embarrassment.*"

"No, I'm not, I'm a boy!" he hollers back.

"A *crabby* boy," I mock.

"I AM *NOT CRABBY*!"

Other shoppers look over. The sales clerk clears her throat loudly.

Mom snatches the tiara piñata from my hands. "No one is buying anything today." She takes us by the arms and starts to lead us away. "I'll buy the piñata for your party next week, Vicka, when I get the rest of the supplies."

"But that's the last tiara on the shelf! It might be *gone* next week!" My voice sounds as high and jagged as Lucas's did earlier. Now I'm the one causing a scene!

"Vicka," Mom says, "calm down. I'll ask the clerk to put it on hold for us. You wait with Lucas, okay?"

I cross my arms, half angry, half embarrassed for acting like a kindergartner. "Okay," I mumble.

Mom forces a tired smile. "That's my girl." She looks at Lucas. "I'll just be a minute, then we'll stop at the food court for ice cream."

Lucas's red-rimmed eyes brighten. "Can I get sprinkles too?"

"Sure," Mom says. "Sprinkles it is."

Lucas jumps up and down excitedly. He grabs my hand and pulls me out into the mall. "Follow me, Vicka!" he shouts. "I know the way!"

A minute later, Mom and I are following Lucas as he skip-hops down the wide mall walkway. We laugh together as Lucas announces to everyone who passes by, "*I* get ice cream! With sprinkles!"

Mom gives my shoulders a hug as we walk along. "You were a big help to me back there, promising to take Lucas to the library, and agreeing to wait for the piñata," she says. "That was very grown-up of you. *Gracias.*"

"You're welcome," I reply.

Mom tucks the gift for Annelise inside her big tote bag. My purse is tiny compared to hers. Still, I stand a little taller and notice we are almost the same height now.

I really *am* growing up!

Chapter 2

Candy Crush

The GlamaRama! is near the food court, so Mom and Lucas get in line for ice cream while I pause to look through the store's big front window. Since the GlamaRama! is new, Bea made me promise not to go inside without her. We're BFFs, so we *always* keep our promises to each other.

Even though Bea and I aren't crazy about spending a whole Saturday with bossy Annelise, we are super excited to be going to her party at the GlamaRama! Our parents won't let us wear makeup yet, so we're really jazzed to get glammed up for a day.

Lots of girls are in the store, browsing the shelves

of hair and makeup products. Some are watching music videos on a giant flat screen. Others are sitting in front of a big movie-star mirror, getting makeovers by the GlamaRama! staff. Racks of glittery costumes stand near a doorway marked Glam Cam Studio. Annelise told us about the makeover themes — Divine Divas, Space Odyssey, and Jungle Bash. We'll pick a theme at Annelise's party, get mini-makeovers, and then bling it up with jewelry and costumes for our glamour photo shoot!

Just then, a group of girls bursts out of the store carrying glittery GlamaRama! shopping bags. I recognize some of them from school, but they are older than I am. I'm glad Mom has my gift bag for Annelise — balloons aren't nearly as glamorous as glitter!

The girls are so busy chatting with each other, they don't see me standing there and nearly knock me off my sneakers!

"Thanks for stopping by!" a tall, lean man calls

after them. "Have a *spa*-tacular day!" He waves to the girls as they head off in different directions around the mall. He's wearing a GlamaRama! shirt and name tag.

Hi! My name is:
LARS
Be beautiful!

Lars taps the screen on the tablet he's holding, then goes back into the store.

"Hey, Vicka!" a boy's voice calls out. "Over here!"

I look toward the food court. There, waving from a Boy Scouts booth, is my crush, Drew.

Yikes!

For a second, I think about ducking into the GlamaRama! to avoid him, even though I like when he notices me. But I always blush and get tongue-tied when he talks to me, which is embarrassing. It's easier to like a boy from a distance.

But I promised Bea I wouldn't go into the store without her, so escaping in there is not an option.

Stay calm, I tell myself. *He's just a boy.*

I walk over to the Boy Scouts booth. Another boy from my class, Henry, is there too. Both he and Drew are wearing their Boy Scout uniforms. Henry is sitting down, playing a game on his phone. Naturally, he doesn't even look up. When you are unfortunately average, like me, it's easy to be ignored.

But Drew steps up to the table he's standing behind and smiles at me, which instantly makes me feel *above* average.

"Hi, Drew," I say, willing my cheeks to stay in the pink zone.

"Hi, Vicka," Drew says. "Would you like to buy a candy bar? They're only a dollar each." He points at the boxes of candy that sit on the table. "We've got three kinds — milk chocolate, dark chocolate, and caramel."

I still have two dollars in my purse. Mom suggested I buy candy for Annelise's gift bag. I could get a candy bar for her, and one for Lucas to make up for my crabby comments to him earlier. I won't have enough money to buy one for myself, but that's okay. Being generous feels almost as good as eating chocolate!

"I'll take two," I say to Drew. "One for my brother, and one for Annelise. It's her birthday on Saturday."

"Cool," Drew says. "Which kind do you want for your brother? Milk chocolate is *sweet* . . ." he explains, pointing to the first box of candy, ". . . dark chocolate is *bitter* . . . and caramel is my *favorite*."

"I'll take caramel," I say quickly.

"Good choice," Drew replies, taking a caramel candy bar from one of the boxes. "And how about *dark* chocolate for Annelise?" he continues. "Bitter, to match her personality."

He snickers. I grin.

Undoing the big, plastic button on my sparkly felt purse, I hunt for my two dollars. I don't have a wallet, so I always just shove my money to the bottom. I made the purse from a kit last summer. Bea made one too. At first, I thought it was super cute, but now it seems kind of babyish. I wish I'd asked Bea if I could borrow one from her sister, Jazmin, but I didn't know I'd see Drew today.

As I dig through my purse, two packs of gum, a tube of lip gloss, and Dad's old flip phone fall out onto the table. *¡Uf!*

Drew laughs. "What else ya got in there, Vicka? A basketball? Bicycle, perhaps?"

"No," I mumble. "I don't play much basketball. And I keep my bike in my back pocket."

Drew chuckles, which makes me feel a little better about my dorky purse. I fish out my two crumpled dollar bills and hand them to Drew.

"Hi, Drew!" two voices singsong behind me.

Glancing over my shoulder, I see two of the older girls who were at the GlamaRama! earlier. Their glittery shopping bags dangle from their slim wrists. Frothy drinks are in their hands. They hurry up to us in a whoosh of espresso-scented air.

The girls greet Henry too. He glances up and grunts, which is how boys say, "Hi!" to pretty girls.

They turn their attention to Drew. One has long, silky-straight hair. The other girl's hair is cut short with cool purple highlights. "Look at you in your little uniform!" the girl with long hair teases Drew.

Drew grins. "At your service, ladies," he says, saluting.

Since Drew is one of the most popular boys at my school, everyone loves talking to him. The girls listen as Drew tells them about the candy bars. "I recommend milk chocolate for you two," he tells the girls. "They're the *sweetest*."

The girls giggle, handing over their money. One of them takes body spritz from her shopping bag and sprays it on Drew's shirt! She laughs hysterically as Drew sniffs his sleeve and makes a face.

"What's wrong?" she asks. "Honeysuckle is the *sweetest*!"

Both girls laugh and start chatting it up with

Drew. They aren't tongue-tied at all, even though it's obvious they like him.

I scramble to stuff my belongings back inside my dorky purse. As I do, my unfortunately average flip phone starts ringing.

¡Uf! Bad timing, Bea! I grab the phone and turn it off. The girls look at me. The one with purple hair says, "Oh, wow, my grandma has that *same* phone!" She doesn't say it in a mean way, but still, it stings.

I have the same phone as her abuela? ¡Ay!

Quickly, I cram the phone into my purse, along with the candy bars I bought and all my other stuff.

Now the purse bulges weirdly, like a cartoon fish that just ate an elephant. It's so stuffed, I can't get the button to clasp.

"Gotta go," I mumble, shoving the purse under my arm and turning to leave. I feel *much* younger than I did a few minutes ago.

Victoria Torres, Total Geek!

I'm zipping toward the food court, where Mom

and Lucas have just set three ice cream sundaes on one of the tables, when I hear my name being shouted again. "Hey, Vicka! Wait up!"

I turn around just as Drew runs up to me with another candy bar. "I forgot to tell you," he says. "It's buy two, get one free." He puts the candy bar in my hand. "This one is *milk* chocolate," he says. "I thought *you* might like the sweet kind."

He smiles at me and starts backing away. "See you at school?"

All I can do is nod.

Drew smiles bigger, then hurries back to the booth.

I stand there for a moment, my knees feeling like jelly doughnuts inside my faded jeans.

Then turning on the heel of my lace-up sneakers, I clutch the world's *sweetest* candy bar to my chest and float the rest of the way to the food court.

Chapter 3

Slam!

"He gave the candy bar to me," I tell Bea over video-chat after we get home from the mall. Dad let me borrow his phone to call her, since my old flip phone doesn't do anything fancy. "That counts as a present from a boy, doesn't it?"

"It totally counts," my BFF tells me matter-of-factly. Bea doesn't mess around when it comes to boys. She studies them like a math problem. "He likes you, Vicka."

I nervously pet Poco, who is snoozing on my lap. My stomach squirms a little. "But he told the other girls about the sweet chocolate too," I tell Bea. "He jokes like that with everyone. It doesn't mean he likes me."

"He does," Bea says. "I'm sure of it. Do you want me to ask him?"

"No!" I shout. Poco jumps, then settles back to sleep. "I would die of embarrassment if he didn't like me back!" Secretly, I would die even more if he *did*. What do you do if a boy actually likes you? I have no idea.

"Okay, okay!" Bea says. "Chill. I won't say a word. Now tell me everything about the GlamaRama!" Bea scoots toward her phone camera so that all I can see are her big, brown eyes framed by dark curly hair. "Is it as glamorous as we were hoping?"

"More," I say.

Bea squeals. "Tell me!"

"Everything *glitters*," I say.

"Oh!" Bea gasps. She loves sparkly things. "I can't wait for Annelise's party! I hope she picks Divine Divas for our photo shoot. We can go bonkers with the bling!" Bea messes with her hair. "I might even wear a tiara!"

"That reminds me," I say. "I found the perfect piñata for my birthday party! It's shaped like a tiara. Mom is going to buy it next week. You're coming to my party, right?"

"Of *course* I'm coming!" Bea exclaims. "Your parties are the best! I love how your family jokes around and sings songs. Your grandma always does that crazy dance! Are you doing anything special with her this year? I was so jealous last year when you went to that fancy restaurant in the city and saw that play."

Besides a party, Abuela and I do something together, just the two of us, to celebrate our birthday. "She hasn't mentioned anything to me yet," I reply. "Maybe we'll —"

The front door flies open. I look over from the living room couch. Poco startles again. This time he jumps to his tiny feet, barking ferociously. He dreams of being a guard dog.

My sister, Sofia, walks in and gives the door a shove.

Slam!

"What was that?" Bea asks.

"The front door," I say.

"Lucas?" Bea wonders.

I shake my head. "Sofia."

Bea makes a face. "But she doesn't slam things."

"Wanna bet? She's fourteen now. Slamming is her new talent. Gotta go."

I turn off the phone just as Sofia storms past. "What's wrong?" I ask.

"Nothing!" she yells, heading for the stairs.

Stomp!

STOMP!!

STOMP!!!

Poco hops down from my lap and hides under the couch. "Some guard dog you are," I tell him.

Dad emerges from the kitchen, a cup of tea in one hand and a magazine tucked under his elbow. "It doesn't sound like *nothing* to me," he says, taking a sip of tea.

Sofia stops at the top of the stairs and turns to glare at us. "If you must know," she says, "Mom just *ruined* my life! *Forever!*" Then she bursts into tears and charges to her bedroom.

SLAM!

The front door opens again. Mom hurries in. "Where's Sofia?" she asks.

Dad points his teacup toward the stairs.

"I wouldn't go up there, if I were you," I say, stepping up to Mom. "She's in one of her grizzly bear moods."

"Rumor has it you've ruined your eldest daughter's life," Dad says. "*Forever.*"

Mom sighs. "Joey, from down the street, invited Sofia over to watch a movie. But his parents aren't home, so I said it would have to be another time."

Dad nods in agreement.

"Sofia stormed off before I could suggest they

watch a movie here instead. Poor Joey was left standing there with me, the evil mother. He finally wandered away."

Mom looks up the stairs again. "I should talk with her."

"Later," Dad suggests. "I'll go up in a bit and test the waters." He takes another sip from his cup.

Mom smiles with relief. "Thanks," she says. Her eyes look tired. "I'm going to take a bath. A *long* bath."

Dad nods. "You do that. I'll hold down the fort."

"Why was Sofia so mad?" I ask Dad as Mom heads upstairs. "She doesn't even *like* Joey Thimble."

"I wouldn't be so sure," Dad replies. "That was a lot of door slamming and foot stomping over someone she doesn't like."

"Here's your phone back," I say, holding Dad's phone out to him.

"Keep it," he says. "I just remembered — Abuela called earlier. She wants you to call her back."

I brighten. "Maybe she's planning our birthday!"

"Could be," Dad says, carrying his tea to the living room and sitting down in the recliner. "Say hi for me."

I dash up to my room, dialing Abuela's number on the way.

"Victoria!" Abuela says a minute later. "I've been thinking about you. Our birthdays are just around the corner."

"I know!" I say excitedly as I hop onto my bed. "I found a piñata at the mall today. It's shaped like a queen's tiara."

"That sounds perfect for our party!" Abuela exclaims. "Did you know I was once a queen?"

I gasp. "You were? Really?"

Abuela chuckles. "Yes, *really*. I was the homecoming queen at my high school. I wore a pretty tiara and rode around town in the back of a red convertible! Your grandfather was king. We went to the homecoming dance together, and we've been dancing together ever since. Nothing makes us prouder than seeing what a fine young lady you're growing into. Twelve years completed! That's special."

I sigh romantically, thinking of Abuela getting swept off her feet by my grandfather at the homecoming dance. I wonder if I'll go to a dance someday. Maybe with Drew!

"I'll bake a special cake, just for you, Vicka," she says. "Triple layer, decorated with a crown! We need to plan our special outing too. See another play? Go to a museum?"

"Whatever you want, Abuela! I like surprises!"

When I get off the phone, I hear Dad talking quietly with Sofia in her bedroom. It sounds like she is crying.

Then I hear pounding coming from down the hall. I look out of my bedroom and see Lucas hammering his fist against the bathroom door.

"Mom?". . . *pound, pound, pound* . . . "Mom?" . . . *pound* . . . "Are you in there?" . . . *pound pound* . . . "Hey, Mom?"

"Lucas!" Mom shouts. "I am taking a bath. If you need something, ask Dad."

"Oh," Lucas says. "But, hey, Mom? Remember how you said we could visit the hermit crabs again? I was thinking now would be a good time."

"Now is *not* a good time, Lucas," Mom calls from the other side of the closed door. "It's late. The hermit crabs are sleeping."

Lucas thinks this through. "But I don't mind if they're sleeping. I just like to look at them."

"No, Lucas. Not today."

Lucas slumps. He kicks the door, then stomps away.

Sofia's bedroom door opens. Dad comes out, grabs a box of tissues from the linen closet, and goes back in.

¡Uf! My family is a mess lately. Thank goodness I have school tomorrow and Annelise's party on Saturday. I'll be able to get away from all the drama!

Chapter 4

Mirror, Mirror on the Wall...

Telling Abuela about the tiara piñata really has me thinking about my birthday party. On Friday morning, I write *piñata* on the shopping list Mom sticks to the refrigerator with a smiley face magnet. Then I draw a tiara next to the word so she'll remember which one I want! We'll need other things for the party too, like paper plates, cups, and ice cream to go with the crown cake Abuela promised to bake. Maybe we could even get tiaras like the ones I saw at the GlamaRama! I doodle a few more suggestions on Mom's shopping list, then fly out the door to school.

Fortunately, Bea and I have last names that are close to each other in the alphabet — Torres and Topper. We almost always stand next to each other in line or sit in the same row in class. Our cubbies were by each other in Pre-K. That's when we met. We've been best friends ever since.

Today, Bea and I are speed-walking to art. We beat the bell with time to spare! We slip into chairs at a table where our friend Jenny is sitting.

"Hi," Bea and I say to Jenny.

"Hi," Jenny replies. Usually, she is very smiley, but today she looks a little down in the dumps.

"Is something wrong?" I ask. "I haven't seen you all morning."

"I had a dentist appointment," Jenny explains. "They pulled two of my baby teeth to make room for the big ones to come." Jenny opens her mouth to show us two gaps on either side of her front teeth.

"Ouchies!" Bea says.

"It didn't really hurt," Jenny says. "The teeth were

tiny and already loose. But now I look like a jack-o'-lantern!" Jenny grimaces. "I have to get *braces* soon."

"It won't be so bad," Bea says encouragingly. "My sister has braces. She gets to pick pretty colors for the bands, like lime green and magenta!"

"Those are two of my favorite colors," Jenny says, "but there's nothing *pretty* about braces."

I squeeze Jenny's arm in a comforting way. "You have the best smile of any of us," I say. "After you get your braces off, it will be even better!"

Jenny starts to smile, but then stops herself. "Until then, my smile is on vacation," she says. "I may as well not even go to Annelise's party tomorrow. I'll look like the Great Pumpkin in all the glamour photos."

"Don't be silly," I say. "You have to come to her party! It wouldn't be the same without you. And the photos will be the best part! The store has tons of glittery jewelry and costumes. We are guaranteed to be *beautiful* with all that glam!"

Jenny cheers up a little. Bea gets her to pose as she

draws Jenny's picture in her sketchbook. Even though Jenny keeps her mouth closed, Bea draws her with a big, beautiful smile!

I wonder if I'll have to get braces someday to go along with my glasses. My teeth are a little crooked, and I still have baby teeth too! My mouth better catch up to the rest of me soon. I'm almost twelve. That's just one year away from being a teenager. It would be unfortunate to still have baby teeth when I'm that old.

Our art teacher, Mr. Tate, calls for everyone's attention. Mr. Tate is not only the middle school art teacher; he is also the high school football coach. He's big, like a football player. He always has a scruffy beard, like my dad does on the weekends. At first, I was afraid of him because he looks so big and his voice is loud and often sounds grumpy. But then one day in art class we were drawing some fruit Mr. Tate had set on a table at the center of the room — apples, oranges, a pear, and a banana.

When Mr. Tate came around to check our work, he stopped and looked at my sketch of the pear. He said, "Now *that's* a pear. You're doing a good job of shading it, Vicka. It's the shadows that make a picture come to life."

Ever since that day, art has been my favorite class! And Mr. Tate isn't so scary, even though he still sounds gruff. Maybe I'll be an artist someday. I already want to be a space explorer. And I want to study dolphins. Sometimes everything seems so interesting it's hard to choose. I guess I'll just be very busy when I grow up!

Mr. Tate begins today's class with a slideshow of famous artists' self-portraits. "You kids think your generation invented the *selfie*?" He shakes his head. "Wrong. These guys did." He starts clicking through paintings by lots of artists. I've heard of some of them — Vincent Van Gogh, Norman Rockwell, and Pablo Picasso. We even have a Picasso calendar on our refrigerator. Some of his paintings look like real people. But others look like Lego people — square heads, triangle bodies, rectangle arms and legs. Mom likes Picasso's real people best. Dad likes the block people. I am somewhere in the middle. I like both styles.

But now, Mr. Tate is talking about an artist I've never heard of before. "Frida Kahlo was a famous artist from Mexico," Mr. Tate explains. Her self-portrait really catches my eye. Her hair is brown, like mine. She drew her eyebrows super dark and thick. At first, it makes me think she's angry, but when I look into her eyes, she seems thoughtful and wise. It makes me realize that first impressions aren't always the ones that last. I think her self-portrait is beautiful, even though some of the kids are laughing about it. "Unibrow," Henry says, snickering.

After the slideshow, Mr. Tate has us open our sketchbooks. He sets up a few mirrors on the tables. "Your turn," he says. "Draw a selfie that shows us who you are, not just how you look."

Jenny squirms next to me. I can tell she doesn't want to see her reflection until her teeth look good again.

Some of the boys are snickering again. Henry picks up one of the mirrors and gazes into it like a beauty queen. "Mirror, mirror on the wall," he says in a girlie voice, "who's the fairest of them all?"

His buddies crack up.

Mr. Tate puts a big, solid hand on Henry's shoulder. "Mr. Anderson," he says to Henry, "time to buckle down and start drawing."

Henry sets down the mirror and picks up his drawing pencil.

I look at my reflection in the mirror that Bea and I are sharing. I draw a circle for my face. Two eyes. A pair of glasses. A nose. A mouth. But it could be anyone's face. What will make it mine?

"Don't forget the shadows," Mr. Tate tells the class. "They will give your picture depth."

I add some shading by the bridge of my nose and

under my chin. The shadows help my self-portrait look like a real face, but it still doesn't look like me.

I think about Frida Kahlo's selfie. Even though I've never met her, I feel like I know who she is because of how she painted her picture.

I turn the page and start over. When the bell rings, I close my sketchbook and tuck away my drawing pencil. *My* selfie is *un*fortunately *un*finished.

Chapter 5

O, Brother!

Annelise, Grace, and Katie meet up with Bea, Jenny, and me for lunch.

"You guys are still coming to my party, right?" Annelise asks as we sit down at our usual table.

"Yes," I reply. "Why wouldn't we?"

Annelise lifts her narrow shoulders. "Plans change. And since I'm having the *deluxe* party, the GlamaRama! is reserving chairs at the makeover mirror especially for *me* and my guests." She bites a baby carrot in half. "We'll meet at the mall. *Don't* be late."

"Even without the reservation there would be plenty of room for us," I say. "I was at the GlamaRama!

yesterday, and there's a whole row of makeover chairs."

"Duh, I know that," Annelise replies. "I went there with my mother when we scheduled the party. They had to let us in through a *special* door because the shop hadn't even opened yet."

Jenny rolls her eyes at Annelise's bragging. "Was it the *servants'* entrance?" She cracks a smile.

Annelise narrows her eyes at Jenny. "No, it was the *staff* entrance." Then she zeros in on Jenny's mouth. "Too bad the GlamaRama! doesn't do *teeth* makeovers."

Jenny stops smiling.

Annelise turns to me. "If you were at the GlamaRama! yesterday, how come you still look so ordinary? Didn't you get a makeover?"

"Nope," I say. "I just walked past the store after buying your *birthday present*." I know telling Annelise this will drive her crazy with curiosity. But it serves her right, for making fun of Jenny's teeth.

Annelise gasps. "What did you buy? Tell me!"

I pretend to lock my lips and toss away the key.

Annelise growls like my grizzly-bear sister. "You are a *meanie*, Victoria Torres!" she wails.

"Takes one to know one," I reply, popping a chicken nugget into my mouth.

Annelise squints.

Jenny snickers.

Bea licks ketchup from her fingers. "I know one thing Vicka got at the mall."

"What?" Grace and Katie ask at the same time.

"Tell me!" Annelise insists.

Bea's eyes crinkle with mischief. "A *candy bar*," she says.

I give Bea a sharp nudge with my elbow.

"I don't care about a *stupid* candy bar!" Annelise says. "All I care about is my *present!*"

Bea rubs her arm where I nudged her, laughing. "Be nice to me, Vicka, or I won't give you *your* birthday present next week!"

"It's your birthday too?" Jenny asks. She moved to Middleton this summer, so we haven't celebrated our birthdays together before. "Are you having a party?"

I nod. "My family always has a party for my grandmother and me. We have the same birthday."

"That's cool," Grace says.

"Family parties are a *borefest*." Annelise chomps another carrot. "I only put up with them for the presents."

Bea frowns. "Vicka's family parties are the best! There's always a piñata, and her grandma does this crazy birthday dance." Bea waves her arms in the air, like Abuela does, while Annelise rolls her eyes and chews her cud. "Oh! Tell them about biting the cake, Vicka! That's my favorite part!"

"Tell us!" Jenny, Grace, and Katie insist.

"It's just another one of our family traditions," I say, glancing at Annelise. She's making a big deal of yawning now, like my whole *life* is a *borefest*. "After I blow out the candles on my cake, everyone starts chanting, *'¡Mordida, mordida, mordida . . . !'* which means *bite* in Spanish. They won't stop until I put my hands behind my back and bite into my birthday cake. As I do, someone — usually my dad or one of my uncles — pushes my face into the frosting, glasses and all!"

Grace and Katie gasp. *"Ewwww!"*

Jenny laughs. "That sounds hilarious!"

"It *is* funny," I reply. "And yummy!"

Annelise scoffs. "Do you play Pin the Tail on the Donkey too? And get birthday spankings?"

Grace and Katie exchange glances. Then they burst out laughing along with Annelise. Even though I like Grace and Katie more than Annelise, sometimes they take her side.

"It's not a kiddie carnival," I reply in defense of my family. Even though, secretly, today my family's traditions do sound a little babyish, even to me.

"Don't listen to Annelise," Bea tells me as we walk home from school later that day. "If she had a family that was half as fun as yours, she'd be begging to come to your party."

"I love my family," I reply. "But maybe twelve is too old for goofy games and dances."

Bea shakes her head. "Annelise thinks she's a know-it-all, but she doesn't know everything. Not even a GlamaRama! party can beat your family parties."

I smirk. "How would you know? We haven't been to a GlamaRama! party yet."

"I'll know tomorrow," Bea says matter-of-factly. "Do you want to ride with me to the mall? I could ask Mom to take us a little early so we can walk around for awhile." Bea grins. "Maybe Drew will be there again."

"Hey, that reminds me. Thanks for blabbing all about my candy bar to everyone! You promised to keep it a secret!"

Bea giggles. "I promised to keep your crush a secret, not the *Drew*bar. Did you eat it yet?"

"Are you crazy?" I exclaim. "I'm keeping it forever!"

Bea laughs. "That's going to be one petrified candy bar!"

"I don't care," I reply. "I'm *never* eating it."

As soon as I get home I check the hallway closet for my purse. I left the candy bars in it when I got home from the mall. I want to hide my *Drew*bar under my mattress, for safekeeping.

But my purse isn't in the closet.

Maybe I left it in the living room when I called Bea to tell her about going to the mall.

Lucas is kicked back in the living room recliner, watching cartoons. Poco is snoozing on the couch.

The jacket I wore to the mall is crumpled in a heap under Poco. My purse is lying limply on the rug with all my stuff scattered around it. The purse must have gotten dumped when Poco decided to use my jacket for his doggie bed.

I gather everything up, including the dark chocolate candy bar for Annelise, the caramel for Lucas, and . . . no milk chocolate for me.

I check under the couch for the Drewbar.

But it's not there.

I shake out my purse.

Empty.

I poke around under Poco.

"*Yip?*"

Nothing.

I straighten up and look around the room. "Where could it be?"

Then I hear a sound coming from the recliner.

Crinkle . . . crinkle . . . crinkle . . .

I look at Lucas. He's giggling over the cartoon he's watching, and ripping open a candy bar.

He tosses the wrapper onto the floor.

I read the words printed on it.

MILK CHOCOLATE

"*LUCAS!*" I scream, just as he takes a big bite.

Lunging for my brother, I snatch what's left of the candy from his hand.

"Hey!" Lucas shouts. "That's mine!"

"Not it's not! You took it! From me!"

"Did not!" Lucas grabs the candy bar back. "I found it on the floor, fair and square!" He shoves the entire bar into his mouth!

Grrrr!

Mom is always telling me to put my things away. For once, I wish I would have listened to her. Now my present from Drew is gone! *Forever!*

I grab the crumpled candy wrapper and rush upstairs.

"What's wrong?" Sofia asks, coming down the stairs as I bolt up them.

"Nothing!" I shout, running to my room.

Slam!

With angry tears sizzling in my eyes, I lift the edge of my mattress, and stick the wrapper in. Then I fall onto my bed, weeping hot tears and plotting the murder of my brother. Maybe I'll make Lucas watch while I eat the caramel candy bar I bought for him. That should do him in. And they can't put me in jail for eating candy.

Chapter 6

A Narrow Escape

The next morning, I wake up earlier than usual for a Saturday. I'm too excited to sleep in because today is Annelise's party! GlamaRama! here I come!

I look through my closet, trying to decide what to wear to the party. But nothing looks right. The girls at the mall the other day seemed so grown-up in their layered camis, skinny jeans, and chunky jewelry. I have camis, jeans, and jewelry too, but everything looks very elevenish this morning. I need a wardrobe makeover before I get a glamour makeover!

Sofia isn't into fashion, but she is in eighth grade. Maybe I can "borrow" one of her outfits, like Bea does with Jazmin's stuff. An older sister's outfit is sure to help me look like I'm *almost twelve*, not *still eleven*.

I ditch my closet and sneak to Sofia's bedroom. Very quietly, I tap on her door. *Tap . . . tap . . . tap . . .*

Nothing.

"Sofia?" I whisper.

Still nothing.

I press my ear to the door, listening. All I hear is snoring.

Good.

Opening the door a crack, I peek inside my sister's room. The curtains are closed. The light is dim. A lump on the bed snores on.

I tiptoe to her closet and snatch two camis, a hoodie, and a short skirt I can wear over a pair of my leggings. As long as Sofia doesn't see me before I leave for the party, everything will be *perfect*!

I dash for the door but hit the brakes when I pass by Sofia's desk. Her diary is lying open on it! I can't resist taking a peek.

Leaning in, I see a drawing of a heart. Fancy scrolls and curlicues surround it, like a Valentine. "I never knew Sofia was an artist!" I whisper to myself. "I thought she was just a brainiac."

Inside the Valentine heart, she's printed two sets of initials.

S.T. for Sofia Torres and *J.T.* for . . . Joey Thimble?!

Gasp!

"Dad was right!" I say, with surprise. "Sofia does like Joey!"

I hear a rustling sound behind me and turn just in time to see a ginormous bedhead rise from the shadows.

"*WHAT ARE YOU DOING?!*" Sofia howls. "*GET OUT OF MY ROOM!*"

A pillow flies.

Fwump!

Fortunately, it's fluffy, so it doesn't break my glasses when it hits me.

*Un*fortunately, Sofia is reaching for a book. Hardcover!

"*STOP LOOKING AT MY STUFF!*"

I dash out of my sister's room just as the book crashes against the doorframe.

Whew!

Sisters are dangerous!

I clutch the outfit to my chest and run back to my room to change.

This is going to be an above average day!

Chapter 7

Annelise's Party!

Bea breathes in deeply as we enter the GlamaRama! later on Saturday. *"Ahhhh,"* she sighs, letting out her breath. "If I didn't know better, I'd say we just walked into a candy store."

I close my eyes and sniff the air. "Gummy worms," I say. "That's what glamour smells like."

Just then, Katie, Grace, and Jenny arrive. Annelise and her mother are already inside, checking in with the shop's staff.

"This place is fantabulous!" Grace says, taking in all the bright lights and glitter.

Katie nods in agreement. "Shineyville!"

Jenny looks around too. "I need a pair of sunglasses," she says, shading her eyes. "All the sparkle is giving me a *bling*ache!"

We all laugh at Jenny's funny comment. "Let's check for shades in the Bling Bin," I suggest, pointing to the big basket of makeup and jewelry I saw the other day.

"Annelise told me we get to pick five things from the Bling Bin for our treat bags," Grace says as we walk over to the bin.

"She told me that too," Katie adds. "Like, ten times."

"It comes with the *deluxe* party package," Jenny adds, mimicking Annelise's snooty voice.

Giggling, we all exchange secret glances around the Bling Bin. Everyone knows what a show-off Annelise can be.

We start digging through the sample-size containers of makeup, hair stuff, and jewelry in the Bling Bin. "Here's some shades!" I say, pulling a pair of sunglasses from the bin. Bright pink with glittery gold rhinestones decorating the frames. Jenny tries them on. She looks like a rock star! Gapped teeth or not, her smile is the best.

The other girls huddle up in front of a nearby mirror with Jenny, practicing their supermodel poses for our photo shoot later. I check out their outfits — camis, hoodies, and jeans, just like me! We all look good, and soon we will look even better, all glammed up with makeup and new hairstyles.

"Enjoy the party, girls," Annelise's mother says when they rejoin us a minute later. "I'll be shopping in the mall. Call if you need me."

"We won't," Annelise sasses, taking Jenny's sunglasses and trying them on for herself.

"Thank you, Mrs. Cooper," I tell Annelise's mother. Mom reminded me to mind my manners today. But Mrs. Cooper is already halfway across the store, chatting on her phone. She doesn't look back as she leaves the store and disappears into the mall.

"Good morning, glamour girls!" a man's voice says. I turn and see Lars, from the other day. "Are you ready to be beautiful?"

Annelise frowns. "We expect to be gorgeous, not just beautiful. My mother bought the deluxe party package."

Lars taps his tablet screen. "So I see," he says. "Which theme interests you? Divine Divas . . . Jungle Bash . . . or Space Odyssey?"

As Lars mentions each theme, he taps his screen again and again. Pictures of girls dressed up like rock stars, wild queens of the jungle, and star-studded space explorers appear on the big flat screen that hangs above us. All the themes look like fun, but Space Odyssey is the coolest — the girls wear sparkly silver jumpsuits and funky pink moon boots!

"I want Divine Divas," Annelise says, without asking our opinions. Oh well, she *is* the birthday girl. It's only fair she gets to decide how we celebrate.

Bea bounces excitedly. She was hoping for Divine Divas!

"Got it," Lars replies, typing on his tablet. "This way to the Makeup Studio!"

He leads us across the store to the big movie-star mirror. The lights around it are so bright I could use a pair of sunglasses from the Bling Bin right now!

We each grab a seat in front of the mirror. I take off my glasses, then the GlamaRama! staff get busy making us beautiful!

As one of them adds some purple highlights to my hair, the door of the Glam Cam studio opens. Jungle music pours out and mixes with the funky music already playing in the main store. I can see a stage with two cardboard banana trees and lots of fake vines. Toy monkeys hang from them. A woman with a camera looks out from the studio. "Jungle Bash?" she calls out.

A group of girls look over from the costume racks. Their eye makeup is dark and glittery. It makes them look like leopards! Each girl wraps a feathery boa around her neck. One of them is wearing a glittery pink safari hat. Another one is wearing a pair of sparkly binoculars. Two of the other girls slip on tiger-striped vests.

They hurry into the photo studio. The photographer closes the door, and the jungle music fades to a low rumble. Meanwhile, my friends and I add the finishing touches to our *spa*-tacular diva makeovers — bright eye shadow, sparkly blush, and stick-on jewels that add even more glittery glam to our new look. I put on my glasses again and check myself out in the mirror. I look great!

Annelise leads the way to the costume racks. We slip on sparkly vests and frilly skirts over our leggings. Then we grab blingy props — shiny microphones, funky hats, even tiaras! Everyone glams it up. We totally rock as divine divas!

Soon the Glam Cam studio door opens again. The Jungle Bash girls burst out, laughing and chattering like jungle birds. They gather at the check-in counter while Lars shows them pictures from their Glam Cam session on a computer. Everything happens so fast here! One moment we are ordinary girls, and the next we are glamour girls! If only all the changes in my unfortunately average life could be this easy!

"Divine Divas?" The photographer steps out of the Glam Cam Studio again. "I'm just resetting the props for your photo shoot. We'll be ready to rock 'n' roll in a minute!"

We hurry into the photo studio as the photographer rolls the banana trees off to the side and replaces them with a big sparkly arch that looks like it belongs on a concert stage. We gather under it, posing in lots of glamorous ways while rock music blasts and the camera flashes.

"This picture is the cutest thing *evah*!" Grace says as we eat yummy cupcakes in the shop's Party Pit, admiring the photos Lars printed for us and showing each other our Bling Bin treat bags. Mine is bulging with pink nail polish, strawberry lip gloss, a super sparkly locker magnet, and rhinestone-studded sunglasses, which are so much cuter than my regular glasses — we each got a pair!

"Let's all wear our new shades to school on Monday," Jenny suggests.

"We'll be the stars of Middleton Middle School," I add.

Everyone agrees our diva sunglasses will add a lot of glamour to our sixth-grade class!

"Enough chitchat," Annelise says. "Time for presents!" She pulls our gifts toward her like a bear gathering jars of honey.

"Thanks, Vicka!" Annelise says, taking the earrings and bracelet from my gift bag. She puts them on right away, so I know she likes them. Then she takes the candy bar from the bag. "How did you know I *adore* dark chocolate?" she asks.

"Just a hunch," I say, smiling to myself as I remember joking with Drew at the candy booth.

Mrs. Cooper returns as Annelise tears into the gifts from the other girls. "My, don't you girls look gorgeous," she says. "Let me take your picture." She fumbles for her phone.

"Not *now*, Mother!" Annelise says, rudely. "Can't you see I'm opening my presents?!"

Yikes! My mom would not allow me to speak that way to her. But Annelise's mom just replies, "Whatever you want, dear!" Then she wanders toward the store entrance, talking on her phone again.

Everyone gives Annelise fun gifts, which makes me even more excited for my birthday party! Usually, I only invite Bea, but maybe my parents will let me invite other friends this year.

Lars appears with a stack of posters in one hand and a fancy certificate in the other. "Thanks for celebrating your birthday at the GlamaRama!" he says to Annelise. "As part of your *deluxe* party package, you've earned a membership in our Bling of the Month Club!"

Lars gives Annelise the certificate, then gets busy hanging up posters around the store.

We crowd in, reading Annelise's certificate.

CONGRATULATIONS!

You are now an official member of the

BLING OF THE MONTH CLUB!

Compliments of the
GlamaRama! Beauty Boutique

Where girls are beautiful!

"That is so cool!" Grace tells Annelise. "You'll get to pick something from the Bling Bin every month for a whole *year*!"

"Lucky you, Annelise!" I exclaim. "You'll be the Queen of Bling at school this year!"

Annelise soaks up all our compliments. Then she says to me, "You could be a bling queen too, Vicka, if you had your birthday party here. And make sure to tell your parents that you want the deluxe package, like *me*."

"Do it, Vicka!" Katie says. "We'll all come!"

I look around the group. Everyone is nodding excitedly. Even Bea seems anxious for me to have my party here. I guess all the bling has gone to her head too!

"That would be überfun," I say, "but my parents are already planning a family party for my grand-mother and me. It's a Torres family tradition."

"So?" Annelise says. "Just have two parties. I always do. One for my family and one for my friends."

She glances across the store at her mother, then back at us. "*Twice* the presents!"

All the girls start talking at once about how much fun it would be to have another party here.

I had never even considered having two birthday parties, but it would solve everything. If I *did* have two parties, I would get to do all my favorite family traditions, but I wouldn't have to worry about my friends seeing me act all silly. After all, I'm not a little kid anymore. I'm almost twelve!

Plus, if I have a *deluxe* party, we can do the Space Odyssey theme! And I'll be a member of the Bling of the Month Club, just like Annelise. Then I will *really* shine all year!

Lars circles back and hangs up his last poster. "You won't want to miss this *spa*-tacular event," he says before returning to the front of the store.

"Look, you guys!" Grace says, reading the poster. "Queen Callie Flower is coming to the GlamaRama! for one day only!"

Meet local celebrity
~ CALLIE FLOWER ~

Winner of the state
Teen Queen Pageant!

PRIZES!
PHOTOS WITH
QUEEN CALLIE!
MALL PARADE!

One lucky girl
crowned
Queen-for-a-Day!

"Queen Callie rocks," Katie says. "I saw her in a parade last summer."

Grace nods. "Me too! She's super pretty!"

Annelise flicks back her diva hair. "She can't be as pretty as me."

Now Bea jumps into the conversation, pointing at the poster. "Look at the date she'll be here, Vicka! Your birthday!"

I read the date printed at the bottom of the poster. Bea is right! Queen Callie Flower will be at the GlamaRama! for one day only . . . on *my* birthday!

Bea hops up and down excitedly. "Sweet! She's going to pick a queen for the day. It's sure to be you, Vicka. You will be the birthday girl!"

"Or me," Annelise says. "The birthday girl's BFF!"

"Count me in," Grace adds. "Queen Callie's Bling Mobile is the cutest thing *evah*! I saw it at the parade. It's a blinged up golf cart — purple sparkles and pink flowers! Maybe she will give all of us a ride!"

I gasp, thinking what that would be like. Wearing a *real* tiara, just like Abuela, and riding with my friends in a parade! Lots of shoppers would stop to watch as we pass by. Maybe Drew will be selling candy bars again! I'm sure to get his attention. It's impossible not to shine when you are perched on a glittery golf cart!

"It's settled then," Annelise says matter-of-factly. "Vicka is having her birthday party at the GlamaRama! All in favor say, 'Aye.'"

"Aye!" we all shout at the same time.

A pretzel-scented gust of air greets us as we burst out of the GlamaRama! a few minutes later.

Wow! Things really do change fast in sixth grade. Just a few hours ago I walked into the mall as Victoria Torres, Unfortunately Average.

But now, I'm walking out as Victoria Torres, Future Birthday Queen!

This will be my best birthday *evah*!

Chapter 8

A Big Decision

Lucas is sitting like a sad garden gnome on our front porch when Bea's mom drops me off after the party. He glances up when I sit down next to him, but he doesn't even notice my purple diva hair or the rhinestone sunglasses I'm wearing instead of my regular glasses.

"Oh, hi, Vicka," he says. "I'm having a time-out."

"How come?" I ask my little brother.

"Mom is mad at me because I screamed and cried at the grocery store when she said we didn't have time to visit the hermit crabs today." He sighs and rests his chin in his hand. "She still thinks I'm too little to take care of one, but I'm big now, Vicka, see?" He jumps up and measures himself against the porch railing. "I don't need to stand on my tiptoes anymore to see over the top!"

"Mom and Dad don't mean you're not *tall* enough for a pet," I say. "A pet takes a lot of work. You have to remember to feed it, play with it, and clean up after it every day."

"I can do *all* those things," Lucas says, tears brightening his eyes. "But no one will believe me!"

"Then you'll have to prove it," I say.

Lucas sits down again. "How?"

I think for a moment. "You could take care of Poco all by yourself for awhile. But you have to remember to feed him, take him for walks, and play with him all on your own. After you show Mom and Dad that you can do that, try asking them for a hermit crab again. But if they still won't let you have one, you cannot throw a tantrum. That will only convince them you're still not ready."

"Okay, Vicka," Lucas says. "No tantrums." He hops up and looks around the yard. "Where's Poco? I want to start taking care of him right away!"

Lucas runs off, shouting Poco's name. I go inside the house, looking for Mom. I can't wait to show her how glamorous I look and to tell her I want a deluxe birthday party of my own!

"Wow, look at you!" Mom says a few minutes later. She stops putting away groceries while I do a step-turn, showing her my new look. "*Very* glamorous. I suppose there will be no living with you now."

I drape my arm across the groceries. "I suppose not," I reply.

Mom laughs. "Look what I found at the store, Drama Queen," she says, reaching into one of the grocery bags. "Paper plates and napkins that match the tiara piñata you want for your party!"

Mom pulls two packages from the bag. The plates

and napkins are decorated with super cute jeweled crowns. "Do you like them?"

I nod. "Yes, but . . ."

Mom smiles. "Great!" she continues. "I'll buy the piñata next week when I'm at the mall for a haircut. Let me know how many friends you plan to invite so we have enough treats for the piñata. Bea, of course, but anyone else? Maybe that Jenny girl you've been talking about? And Annelise, since she just invited you to her party. Oh, that reminds me, Abuela wants you to call her. I talked with her today, and she's very excited because there's a special program at the aquarium in the city on your birthday! You'll get to go behind the scenes and see how they take care of the animals. You'll even get to feed a dolphin!"

"*On* my birthday?" I ask.

Mom nods. "You can go to the program in the morning and be back in time for your party in the afternoon. Sound good?"

Yikes!

I slump against the kitchen counter. I love the aquarium, and I'm dying to feed a dolphin! But I want to celebrate with my friends at the GlamaRama! Plus, Queen Callie will be there on my birthday. I'm counting on being her queen for the day!

"Did Abuela buy the tickets yet?" I ask, desperately hoping she hasn't. Maybe we could go to the aquarium program a different day.

"I think so. Why?" Mom studies me for a moment. "Is something wrong, Vicka? Don't worry, you'll get back from the city in plenty of time for your party."

"I'm not worried about that," I say. "It's just that we had so much fun at Annelise's party today! There are different themes, and I want to do Space Odyssey more than anything! We'll get to wear the cutest moon boots for our photo shoot! Plus, if I have a *deluxe* party, like Annelise, everyone gets cupcakes and treat bags filled with makeup and jewelry, and I'll get to be a member of the Bling-of-the-Month Club!

Oh, and a *real* queen will be there on my birthday! There's going to be a parade and all my friends think I will get picked to be her Queen-for-a-Day!"

I stop talking and catch my breath.

Mom stares at me for a moment, a jar of peanut butter in her hand. "What are you saying, Victoria?" she finally asks. "Don't tell me you're thinking of having a GlamaRama! party for your birthday."

"Yes!" I say. "I am! *Pleeease?* Abuela could exchange the aquarium tickets for another day."

Mom sets down the peanut butter. *Thunk!* "We've already made plans for your family party," she says. "Besides, you love celebrating with Abuela."

"Couldn't we have the family party on a different day?"

Mom's eyes go wide. "*Two* parties?" She shakes her head. "No, Vicka. That wouldn't be fair to Lucas or Sofia. And this *deluxe* party you mentioned sounds expensive. That's something we would have to plan for. Maybe next year."

Next year?!

"But Annelise gets two parties this year!"

Mom starts putting groceries away again. "This isn't a competition, Victoria," she says, crisply. "If you want a mall party *this* year, it will have to be *average*, not deluxe. And you'll have to make a choice: celebrate your birthday *there*, with your friends, or celebrate it here, with your family. *Not both.*"

My mouth drops open. "Glam or fam?"

Mom nods. "Yes," she says firmly. "And let me know your decision soon. I'll have to ask Aunt Selene and Uncle Julio to host a party for Abuela if you decide not to have one here."

Mom turns away again, opening cupboard doors, putting things away, shutting them again.

Slam!

SLAM!

SLAM!!

My shoulders sag under the weight of what Mom just said. What about biting into my cake? And my piñata? And all the silly songs? My heart is tugging in two directions — sad *and* mad — which makes my chest feel like it's going to break apart.

I storm out of the kitchen and march upstairs.

Stomp!

STOMP!

STOMP!!

The family pictures that are hanging along the stairway rattle against the wall with every step.

I slam my bedroom door and fall onto my pillow, crying.

Poco, who loves to nap on my bed, jumps up as soon as I flop down. He whines with concern as I cry. Then he nudges my arm with his pink eraser nose.

I pull him in.

"Mom is being so unfair!" I sob. "Why shouldn't I get two parties? Annelise does! Twelve is a very important year! Doesn't Mom know that? I'm not the youngest in the family. I'm in the *middle*. So why is she treating me like a baby?"

Poco licks away my tears.

I take a deep, ragged breath and scratch his back. We got Poco the year Lucas was born. Abuela took Sofia and me to a carnival. A man was there with performing dogs. The dogs could jump through hoops and dance on their hind legs. One could even play a toy piano! He plunked out the notes with his eraser-pink nose.

The dog show was my favorite part of the carnival. I wished for a pet after that, just like Lucas is wishing for one now. Sofia already had goldfish, but I wanted a puppy! Mom and Dad told me a puppy would be too much work, especially with a new baby in the family. I was so disappointed, just like Lucas.

Not long after that, Abuela came to our house with a little Chihuahua puppy that needed a home. I fell in love with him right away. So did Sofia. Even Mom and Dad softened and said we could keep him. I was so happy! Poco belongs to our whole family, but secretly I think of him as mostly mine.

I roll over on my back and wipe the tears from my eyes. I have a *big* decision to make. Celebrate my birthday with my family and feed a *real* dolphin, or celebrate with my friends and meet a *real* queen.

If I choose family, my friends will be disappointed.

If I choose friends, my family will be sad.

And no matter which one I choose, someone is going to be completely bummed.

Unfortunately, that someone is *me*.

Chapter 9

Abuela to the Rescue

"I should have asked you before I bought the tickets, Vicka," Abuela says after I've calmed down and called her. "But there were only two left for the special program, so I snatched them up! What do you think? Will you go to the aquarium with me on our birthday?"

Fortunately, I'm calling Abuela on my old flip phone, so she can't see me bite my lip nervously. I hate to disappoint her.

"Oh, dear," Abuela says when I don't answer right away. "Something is wrong, Vicka. I can hear it in your silence."

Just like my parents, Abuela can tell when I'm hiding my true feelings.

I force myself to sound upbeat. "No," I say. "I am excited, Abuela. It's just . . . I thought maybe . . . we could go to the aquarium program on a different day? There's a special event at the mall too. My friends and I really want to go, but Mom says I have to choose between a friends party and a family party."

"The aquarium program is sold out, I'm afraid," Abuela says. "But there will be other programs in the future, I'm sure. You are growing up to be your own person, Vicka, with your own interests and dreams. You have completed twelve years! It's time for you to choose your own path."

I feel tears brewing at the back of my eyes again. "I want to celebrate my birthday with my friends *and* with you, Abuela. I *do* want to make my own choices, but I want someone to tell me which choice is *best*."

"You are a smart, thoughtful girl, Vicka. I know you will make the right choice, and I will be happy no matter what it is. Now tell me about this special program at the mall."

I wipe a tear from my cheek and tell Abuela all about the GlamaRama! and how Queen Callie Flower will be there on my birthday.

"Queen Callie?" Abuela says. "I know her! She helped with the book drive at the library last month. She was wonderful. And how exciting for you to meet a queen on your birthday!"

"Queen Callie will pick someone to ride with her in the mall parade," I tell Abuela. "My friends think she will choose me, since I will be the birthday girl."

"Of course she will choose you!" Abuela says, cheerfully. "How could she resist?"

I tell Abuela all about the Space Odyssey theme and that I'm sorry about the aquarium tickets and that Mom is mad at me for wanting to change plans at the last minute.

"Don't you worry about a thing," she says when I finally pause long enough for her to get a word in. "I'll talk with your mother. Lucas might like to go to the aquarium with me. I'll find another way to make your birthday special."

"Lucas would *love* going to the aquarium," I say. "But stay away from the crabs unless you want to deal with a tantrum. He's crab crazy lately."

"Did someone say my name?" Lucas pokes in from the hallway.

"Yes," I reply. "Abuela has two tickets to the aquarium. Do you want to go?"

Lucas jumps up and down. "Yes! Yes! Yes!" he shouts. "When? Now? I have to play with Poco first!"

He races in and scoops up Poco.

"*Woof?*" Poco says, hanging over my brother's shoulder like a sack of gym clothes. Lucas runs out again before I have a chance to tell him the trip is still a week away.

Abuela laughs as we listen to Lucas running down the hall shouting, "Mom! Dad! Abuela is taking me to the aquarium!"

"I think we just gave your brother a present!" she says to me.

"*Sí*," I reply, "and it's not even *his* birthday!"

When I hang up the phone, I'm so relieved that Abuela understands about my wanting a friends party. If only Mom would.

Chapter 10

Glam vs. Fam

The purple highlights are still in my hair on Monday morning.

And Mom is still mad because I keep going back and forth about my party. One minute I'm thinking *family,* and the next minute I'm thinking *friends.*

She's barely talked to me since Annelise's party. And when she does speak, her words are chilly, like sprinkles on an ice cream sundae. Only the sprinkles are not sweet. And the sundae is frozen solid.

Why is she so upset? Doesn't she want me to spend time with my friends?

Everything would be perfect if she'd let me have

two parties — one with my friends on my birthday and one with my family on a different day.

"Don't be an idiot, Vicka," Sofia says as we're both eating breakfast before school. Mom is upstairs, helping Lucas get dressed for the day. Dad is at work. Poco is snoozing off the extra helping of dog food Lucas gave him a few minutes ago. "Mom told me about your glamour party idea. You can go to the mall anytime with your friends. But getting our whole family together to celebrate only happens a few times each year. If there's no party, then no cake. No piñata. No *presents* from all your relatives."

"But if I have my party at the mall, I'll get to meet a real *queen*," I explain. "And maybe ride on her float in a parade. That would be a big deal. Besides, I want to celebrate with my friends."

"Queen *spleen*," Sofia gripes. "And you're not the only one with friends, you know. I've already invited someone to come to the family party. If you change your mind now, I'm going to have to *un*invite him."

I make a puzzled face. "Him?"

Sofia shifts in her chair. "Yes, *him*," she says. "Joey Thimble."

My eyes go buggy. "Why would you invite him to my party? He's never come before. Plus, he barely speaks. And he always smells like pine needles."

Sofia squints. "That's his *cologne*. And I can invite a friend if I want to. Mom said so."

I cross my arms. "Friend . . . or *boyfriend*?"

Sofia narrows her eyes until they are as thin as knife blades. "He's a boy who is my friend, that's all."

"Then why don't you invite him to Abuela's party at Aunt Selene's house instead? You can show him off there, just as well as here."

Sofia growls. "I'm not trying to show him off. Just do what I say, Vicka. If you don't, you'll mess up everything!" She pushes away from her breakfast and nearly stomps poor Poco on her way to the refrigerator.

Mom and Lucas come downstairs. Sofia grabs an

apple from the fridge, and tosses it into her backpack. "Think about what I told you," she says, shooting another look at me as she gathers up her school stuff.

"What did Sofia tell you?" Lucas asks, changing the water in Poco's dog dish. He is really taking this pet thing seriously! I saw him change Poco's water before breakfast too.

Sofia locks eyes with me. I know I'm doomed if I say anything about Joey. "She's helping me with some math homework," I fib. "I have a *big* problem to figure out."

At school, everyone notices my purple diva hair. Even those older girls from the mall see me and say, "Aren't you Drew's friend? Your hair looks fab! And, *ohmygosh*, those are the cutest shades *evah*! You should totally paint your nails to match them."

Wow! Unfortunately-average sixth-grade girls like me almost *never* get compliments from popular seventh-grade girls. I'm glad I tucked away my regular glasses until class, when I'll need them to see the chalkboard. I slather strawberry gloss on my lips and think about the Bling Bin at the GlamaRama! It has lots of nail polish in all kinds of colors. If I have my party there, I will definitely put a bottle of magenta polish in my treat bag!

In art class, we work on our self-portraits. I'm feeling so glamorous, I grab a box of oil pastels and add some color to the sketch I drew of myself the other day. Purple streaks in my hair. Cotton candy pink cheeks. Bright blue eyelids. Strawberry red lips.

Henry glances over as I add some blingy jewelry to my masterpiece.

"Are you joining the circus?" he asks with a snicker. "Vicka the Clown?"

I ignore his immature comment. He wouldn't recognize glamour if it hit him like a pie in the face.

But Drew does. When he walked past me in the hall earlier, he suddenly stopped, turned around, and stared at my purple hair! Then he asked, "New look, Vicka?"

Instead of ducking behind my locker door (which miraculously opened on the first try today — everything works better with glamour!), I flicked back my purple hair and replied with a confident, "Yes!"

I barely even blushed!

Mr. Tate walks over as I put the finishing touches on my blingy self-portrait. He rubs his scruffy chin, studying it for a moment. Then he says, "Good use of color, Vicka, but no shadows this time, eh?"

Mr. Tate moves on down the row. I look at Bea. "Was that a compliment?" I ask my BFF. "Because it didn't exactly feel like a pat on the back."

Bea looks up from her drawing. "It was a mixed message," she explains. "He likes your picture, but . . ."

"But what?" I ask, holding my self-portrait up for her to see.

"But . . . all those bright colors . . ." Bea continues,

studying my selfie, "they're good and everything . . . it's just . . . they kind of hide . . . you."

I double-triple-quadruple check with all the girls at school, to make sure they still want to meet up at the mall next Saturday for my party. I don't dare ask Mom to pick up everyone. She told me I would have to decide by tonight if I'm going to change my party plans.

All of them — Bea, Jenny, Katie, Grace, and Annelise — absolutely, positively, for sure will be there. By the end of the day I've asked them so many times, Bea has started rolling her eyes and calling me Annelise.

Chapter 11

Decision Time

When I get home from school at the end of the day, I absolutely, positively, for sure decide to tell Mom I choose glam over fam.

But first I run upstairs and clean my room.

Then I refold the towels in the linen closet. And wipe toothpaste speckles off the bathroom mirror.

On my way downstairs, I organize the paperclips in Mom's desk and sharpen all her pencils.

And fluff the couch pillows.

Then I set the table for supper even though it's Sofia's turn. And I feed Poco even though Lucas already has, like, three times today.

Poco lifts his head lazily as I walk by his bed with a broom and dustpan, then plops back down, his tummy bulging with all the doggie treats Lucas has been giving him.

I find Mom right before supper and tell her about all the extra chores I did after school. But even after pointing out that I did them without being told — which was a very grown-up thing to do — she just glances up from the potatoes she's mashing and asks, "What have you decided about your birthday party?"

I fiddle with the platter of meatloaf that's sitting on the stove. "I have decided that I am one-hundred percent for sure, probably, going to have my party at the GlamaRama! with my friends, I think."

Mom draws in a deep breath, like a dragon that is waking up from a bad dream, and goes back to mashing the potatoes. *Mash . . . MASH! . . . MASH!!* She drops the masher into the sink — *THUNK!* — and glares at me. "That's your final decision?"

I nod.

Mom picks up the potato bowl and whisks it to the table without looking at me. I follow along with the meatloaf.

"Time to eat!" she shouts out into the house.

I sit down in my usual spot, fold my hands and duck my head.

"What's for supper?" Dad asks cheerfully as he, Sofia, and Lucas come into the dining room.

"*Food*," Mom says as she heads back into the kitchen. The refrigerator door opens, then closes again. *Fwump!* A bag of lettuce is opened. *Rrrrrrip!*

Sofia snorts to herself as she tucks a napkin under Lucas's chin. "And she says *I'm* moody."

Dad looks to me for answers. I just scoop mashed potatoes onto my plate.

My stomach is in knots because I know Mom is upset with my decision. I push food around on my plate, shooting glances at her.

"Look what I made!" Lucas says, breaking the silence a few minutes later. He points to the pile of mashed potatoes on his plate. Six string beans are stuck into it for legs. Two black olives for eyes.

"What is it?" Sofia asks. "A spider?"

"No, Sofia!" Lucas replies. "It's a hermit crab!"

He looks at Mom. "Can I get one, Mom? *Pleeease?* I've been taking extra good care of Poco!"

"No," Mom says, setting down her fork and rubbing the bridge of her nose.

Lucas starts to complain. I nudge his leg under the table and shake my head.

He stops. Sighs. And eats his potato crab.

Wow! No tantrum. That should make Mom happy!

But Mom is *not* happy. Which makes me feel *below* average. She pounces at the salad on her plate like her fork is a claw. When Dad asks her what's the matter, she says, "Nothing," just like Sofia did the other day when *she* was mad.

Mom drops her napkin on top of her unfinished meatloaf. "Sofia," she says, "will you please clear the table when everyone is finished? I have to call all your relatives and *un*invite them to our house for your sister's birthday party on Saturday."

Sofia stops chewing and stares blankly at Mom. "Uh-huh," she finally replies.

"Thank you," Mom says in her abominable snowman voice. She picks up her phone and marches out of the room.

I take a sip of water.

Sofia glares at me. "So you've decided then. No family party."

"Uh-huh," I reply, even though she didn't ask it like a question.

Sofia shakes her head. "Thanks a *lot*, Victoria Torres." She stands up and starts stacking up plates and cups.

"How come everyone keeps saying *thank you*, but no one sounds very thankful?" Lucas asks.

"Things are a little out of sorts tonight, buddy," Dad tells Lucas.

"How come?" he asks.

"Because our sister wants to have a party with her *friends* instead of us!" Sofia butts in.

Mom's voice trails in from the other room as she talks on the phone.

Lucas looks at me. "I don't mind if you have a party with your friends, Vicka. I get to go to the aquarium!" He smiles brightly.

I try to smile back, but it hurts too much. Mom and Sofia are mad at me, and Lucas gets to go to the aquarium instead of me.

Sofia grumbles under her breath as she carries dishes to the kitchen.

"What's for dessert?" Lucas calls after her.

"Nothing," Sofia replies.

Fortunately I have an excuse to get out of the house tonight. Bea and I are going to a concert. Bea takes piano lessons, and if she does extra stuff — like attend concerts or make posters about famous musicians like Beethoven or Mozart — she earns points for cool prizes, like soccer balls and DVDs and funky jewelry and stuff.

"I don't see why Mom is so upset about me wanting to spend my birthday with my friends," I blurt out to Dad as we drive to Bea's house. "Even Abuela agrees that it's my choice."

"That's true," Dad says. "But the way I see it, you've got another choice to make. Choose to stay mad at Mom or choose to apologize."

I gawk at Dad. "Why should I apologize? Mom is the one who is being unfair, not me."

"You changed your mind after all the plans had been made," Dad says. "That wasn't exactly fair either. Mom gets a big kick out of planning birthday parties for you kids. I think it hurt her feelings when you didn't want one this year."

I slump. "I didn't mean to hurt her. I just want to have fun with my friends at the mall."

"I know you didn't mean to hurt her," Dad says.

"Sometimes things just happen. Mom will get over it, but apologizing might help patch things up. It would be the grown-up thing to do."

I sigh. "Okay," I say. "I'll talk to Mom."

Dad smiles. "Bravo." He pulls up to Bea's house. "Shall I wait and drive you girls to the concert?"

"Bea's dad is going to drop us off after we get ready."

Dad makes a puzzled face. "You look ready to me."

I roll my eyes. "Dad, you don't know anything about being a girl. We have things to do before we can go to the concert."

Dad laughs. He leans over and kisses the top of my head. "Have fun, Bonita!" he says.

I give him a hug goodbye. "*Sí*, I will!"

I'm wearing the new dress shoes Mom bought for me when we went school shopping this fall. I like them, but they have flat heels. So do Bea's. This is our first grown-up event since we started middle school. We both want to shine!

"Jazmin is babysitting tonight," Bea tells me as we kick off our flat dress shoes and run up to her room. "We can borrow some heels from her."

Bea is always "borrowing" things from her big sister. Fortunately, she is sneakier than I am and hardly ever gets caught!

I keep watch by Jazmin's bedroom door while Bea slips in. Both of her parents are downstairs so no one knows what we're up to. A moment later, Bea comes out and hands me a pair of super sparkly wedges. She pulls on a pair of spike-heeled boots that come up to the hem of the wool skirt she's wearing.

Jazmin's wedges are a little big for me, but they make me much taller, which makes me feel much older! Bea's boots are big for her too, so she kicks them off and pulls on an extra pair of knee-high socks over her tights.

"Now they fit," Bea says, zipping up the boots and

wobbling around her room. "And if there is a freak blizzard, I won't freeze."

Fortunately, Bea's dad drives us to the concert. He doesn't question our fashionable footwear, so we don't have to explain where we got the shoes. Most dads are great at not noticing glamour.

Clomp, clomp, clomp! Bea and I hurry into the concert hall lobby as fast as we can, which is actually pretty slow because we have to take tiny steps to keep from spraining our ankles. "This way, please," the usher says, giving us programs. He leads us down the auditorium's center aisle, all the way to the front row! "Enjoy the concert, ladies," he says, as Bea and I sit down.

We look at each other and burst out laughing. "He called us *ladies*," Bea says. "Like we're grown-ups!"

"We *are*," I say. "I'll be *twelve* next week. You'll be twelve next month."

"Twelve," Bea says, fanning her face with her program. "Soon we'll be as old as Jazmin and Sofia."

I cross my legs and swing my foot like a clock pendulum, trying to speed up time. The auditorium lights dim. Everything is in shadows, except for my sparkly wedges which glitter like shoe-shaped constellations in a night sky. Everyone starts applauding as the pianist walks on stage and takes her place at the piano. Her dress sparkles just like my shoes! I swing my foot in time to her playing — slowly at first, then faster and faster.

Even though I'm trying to concentrate on the music, my mind wanders to the fight I'm having with Mom. It's been buzzing around my head like a pesky fly since supper.

Dad wants me to apologize to her for changing my party plans because it would be the grown-up thing to do. But as much as I want to be older, sometimes I still feel as little as Lucas.

The music plays faster.

I swing my foot harder.

My sparkly wedge flies right off!

It tumbles into the center aisle.

Clunkity, clunk . . . clunk!

There it sits, glimmering under a stage light, like Cinderella's lost slipper.

Bea gasps when she realizes what has happened.

I freeze.

Fortunately, the auditorium is dim. Even though everyone can see my sparkly shoe, maybe they don't know who it belongs to.

*Un*fortunately, it *clunked* to the floor during a dramatic pause in the pianist's performance. I see her glance my way before continuing.

I sink down into my chair.

Sometimes it's embarrassing to shine!

Chapter 12

Bumblebees and Muskrats

By Friday, my purple hair has faded back to an averagely normal brown. My plan to apologize to Mom has faded too. I promised Dad I would do it, and I always keep my promises. But each time I see Mom, I chicken out! So I've spent the last few days avoiding her, which is hard to do when you live in an average-sized house. Mom is always around. And it's hard to keep a low profile when an imaginary insect is buzzing around your head, reminding you to talk to her. It's the size of a giant bumblebee now.

Buzz . . . BUZZZZ . . . BUZZZZZ . . .

But if I can avoid Mom for just one more day,

then there won't be any reason to apologize because my party will be here! It will be so glamorously great that Mom will see I was right to want a friends party. She will apologize to me for canceling my family party, and everything will be back to normal between us.

I mentally swat at the giant bumblebee and put on my muskrat costume.

The Middleton Middle School football team has a game after school, and I am the team's mascot. I have to wear a big, furry jumpsuit and muskrat mask. The costume is not one bit glamorous, so Bea and I bling it up with barrettes and beaded bracelets. By the time the game starts, I am one glamorous muskrat!

When Jenny, Katie, and Grace see me in my costume, they huddle up around me and shake their pompoms. It's fun having friends on the cheerleading squad!

Annelise is on the squad too, but she doesn't make a big deal about my blingy costume. She just looks at my fur-covered gloves and says, "It must be hard to hold a pair of pompoms when you're wearing those goofy gloves. In fact, maybe you *shouldn't* hold any. They're really only for the cheerleaders, and technically you're not one of us."

Annelise has a way of twisting friendly comments into putdowns. I guess it makes her feel more important when she does this. Which is totally dumb. I'd rather make people feel better about themselves, not worse.

Grabbing a pair of pompoms, I ignore Annelise and hurry out onto the field while the football players are warming up. The fans sitting in the bleachers clap and cheer as I run up and down the sidelines, waving the pompoms, doing goofy jumps and clunky cartwheels. Bea cheers the loudest. "Go, Muskrats!" she shouts from the stands.

Annelise runs out onto the field too. I don't mind *sharing* the spotlight, but she wants to steal it. Instead of cheering with me, she does cartwheels down the sideline, each one perfectly connected to the next like a string of paper dolls.

The crowd applauds politely when she's done, but they don't cheer like they did when I was acting goofy. It's no secret that Annelise wants all the attention for herself. That's the main reason she isn't my *best* friend. True friends don't try to overshadow you.

As the players take the field, I look up into the stands once more before heading to the sidelines. I can't believe what I see.

There's Mom, finding a seat on one of the bleachers! I know she's still mad at me, but she still came to see me cheer at the football game.

Lucas sits down next to her. He sees me and waves.

I wave back.

Mom smiles.

She can't see it, but I'm smiling too, behind my mask.

Mom is at the library for her book club meeting when I get home from the game. I eat quickly, do my homework, and then head to my room for the evening. When I hear her car pull into the drive later, I switch off my light and dive into bed. A few minutes later, I hear her coming upstairs.

I lie very still and take slow, sleepy breaths.

My door creaks open. I sneak a tiny peek and see her standing in my doorway.

I stay quiet.

Mom is quiet too. She watches me for a few moments, then she quietly closes my door.

Riding to the mall on Saturday morning, I sit silently next to Mom. The only sound I hear is the humming of the car and the bleeping of my new fancy phone as I fiddle with the settings. It was my birthday present from my family.

I consider trying out the phone's camera by taking

a picture of Mom, but the imaginary bumblebee that's been bugging me is sitting between us.

Actually, it's morphed into a pterodactyl now. Every time I glance at Mom, it raises its head, blocking my view. It's hard to feel totally excited about your birthday party when an uninvited pterodactyl is tagging along.

"This was supposed to be my best birthday ever," I mumble, clicking off my new phone and tucking it into my pocket. "But it's turning out to be below average. No piñata. No cake. No family."

"Dad made you waffles with ice cream for breakfast," Mom replies. "All is not lost."

I sink lower in the seat.

"Lucas is probably feeding a dolphin right now. *My* dolphin." I look at Mom. "Why didn't you tell me I would be this bummed if I didn't go to the aquarium with Abuela?"

"A little sadness isn't such a bad thing," Mom says, checking her rearview mirror and merging into the other lane. "It reminds us all of how great happiness is."

"*Ugh*, Mom," I say, looking out my window. "That's not the kind of thing a sad person wants to hear."

Mom laughs. "Well, it's true, even if you don't want to hear it. You will be happy again. And, someday, you will feed a dolphin, just not on your twelfth birthday."

I sigh. "Maybe on my thirteenth?"

"Maybe," Mom replies.

We're quiet again, which makes me feel antsy. Plus, the pterodactyl is sharpening its beak on my knee.

I shove it away. Squawking, it crawls into the back seat. I turn toward Mom. "I'm sorry I changed my mind about the party. I know you're mad at me."

Mom squeezes the steering wheel tighter. Then she loosens her grip and pats my knee. "I'm not mad at you," she says. "I was disappointed for awhile, but mostly with myself. It's hard for me to admit that you're growing up. The truth is, sometimes I wish you and Sofia and Lucas would stay little. But no matter how much I wish it, you keep growing!"

She turns on the car's blinker and takes the mall exit. "Lucas is proving he is old enough to have a pet, Sofia is interested in boys, and you want to spend more time with your friends." Mom sighs. "Sometimes growing up feels like growing away."

Mom's shoulders sag a little. I want to reach over and give her a hug, but I'm buckled in. "It's not that I don't want a family party — I *do*. I just wanted a party with my friends *more*."

I sit back again and gaze out the window for a moment. "Birthdays used to be so easy. When people asked me how old I was, I just held up my fingers to show them. But I don't have enough fingers anymore. Now I need ten fingers plus two toes." I sigh. "Growing up is so complicated."

"That's what families are for," Mom says, pulling into the mall's parking lot. "We'll help each other get through the hard stuff this year." She smiles at me. "Happy ten-plus-two birthday, Vicka."

I hold up all my fingers and wiggle my two big toes. *"Gracias,"* I reply.

Chapter 13

Books and Bling

"Look!" Bea exclaims later, as we head down the mall walkway to the GlamaRama! store. "There's Queen Callie's Bling Mobile!"

Bea, Jenny, Katie, Grace, Annelise, and I race over to the sparkly purple golf cart that's parked near the shop's entrance. It's decorated with glittery streamers and balloons. A poster attached to the back of it glitters too.

Her Royal Highness

CALLIE FLOWER
Miss Teen Queen!

"Queen Callie must really love to read!" Jenny says, peering into the golf cart. Crates of kids' books fill the backseat.

"Duh, Jenny," Annelise snips. "She doesn't *read* the books, she gives them away."

"Maybe she does both," I say, coming to Jenny's defense. "My grandmother said Queen Callie helped at the library book drive."

Mom nods. "We were just talking about that at my book club. We're going to make a donation toward her cause."

"But where is she?" Katie asks, looking around.

"Probably getting her nails done," Annelise says. "Or polishing her crown. That's what I would be doing if I were queen."

I look into the GlamaRama!, trying to spot someone wearing a flowing gown and sparkly tiara, but all I see are lots of girls. I'm not the only one who wants to meet a real queen today.

We all go inside. Mom heads over to check us in

while we write our names on slips of paper and put them in a pink safari hat for the prize drawing later. I print my name neatly, fold it in half, and drop it into the hat. I hope I win a prize! But more than anything, I hope Queen Callie picks me to be her Queen-for-a-Day. That would make me feel a lot better about missing my family party.

"I've got good news and bad news," Mom says, rejoining us a minute later. "The good news is you'll each get a mini-makeover, but, unfortunately, there won't be time for a photo shoot today. Not with Queen Callie coming."

Annelise snorts. "At my *deluxe* party, we had a photo shoot."

Bea narrows her eyes at Annelise. "But you didn't have a *queen*."

"Or a parade," Jenny adds, linking arms with Bea and me.

Mom's phone jingles with a text. "It's Aunt Selene. She says they'll wait with the cake if we want to join them after your makeovers." Mom looks up from the screen. "What do you think, Vicka? You were just saying this morning how much you'll miss having cake."

"But what about the parade?" Annelise asks. "I want to ride on the Bling Mobile!"

Everyone looks at me, waiting for my answer. If we go to Aunt Selene's house for cake, my family will sing and act silly. They will chant *mordida* and push my face into the frosting. What will Annelise say then? Something sassy like, "Nice *makeover*, Vicka." She will probably make a big deal about it at school on Monday. Drew is sure to hear, along with all the other kids too.

"Parade," I say.

Annelise smiles.

Mom's jaw tightens, but then she nods. "Parade it is," she says pleasantly. "I'll let Aunt Selene know. Have fun, girls! Meet me here after your makeovers." She heads out into the mall.

"Welcome back, glamour girls!" someone calls out. We turn to see Lars walking up to us. "Ready for another *spa*-tacular day?"

"Yes!" we all shout. Only my shout is below average, because I'm missing my family.

"Which one of you is the birthday girl?" Lars asks.

"Here she is," Jenny says, nudging me forward. "Victoria Torres."

Lars taps his tablet. "Happy birthday, Miss Victoria. There are two parties ahead of you, so hang tight and browse. I'll call your name when it's your turn at the makeover mirror."

I blink with surprise. "You mean I'm not the only one celebrating a birthday today?"

Lars shakes his head. "Lots of girls want to celebrate their birthday with Queen Callie! What could be more *spa*-tacular than that?!"

Lars looks around the shop. "Erika?" he calls out. "Erika Holmes party?"

Several girls look up from the Bling Bin.

Lars smiles at them. "Your turn to be beautiful!" He rushes over to the girls and leads them to the makeup mirror.

I look at my friends. "Queen Callie might choose one of the other birthday girls to be her Queen-for-a-Day."

Bea puts her arm around my slumped shoulders. "No chance," she says, confidently. "You will outshine all of them!"

She pulls me toward to the shelves of beauty products. All the girls follow along. We try samples of hand lotions and body sprays until our group smells like a bag of jelly beans.

"Try this one, Vicka!" Jenny says, holding up a bottle of lotion. "It's called Birthday Cake!"

Jenny squirts the lotion onto my hand. I rub it in. Soon my skin smells as sweet as a chocolate cupcake with sprinkles. The scent is spa-tacular, but it makes me miss my family even more. I wonder if Abuela still made a crown cake. Maybe they will let Lucas bite it for me. He got to go to the aquarium in my place, so he may as well get his face smooshed into my cake too.

I gaze out the GlamaRama! big window, imagining the scene at Aunt Selene's house — everyone taking turns striking a piñata. Uncle Julio and Dad playing guitar and singing while my little cousins dance around. For a moment, I think I see Sofia dash down the mall walkway. That's crazy, of course, because she is celebrating with my family. It's what she wanted, after all.

Music videos are playing on the flat screen, so we grab invisible microphones and sing along like rock stars, dancing around on stage. We're acting just as silly as my family!

"Victoria Torres party?" Lars calls out, looking over the heads of all the girls milling around the shop. "It's time to be beautiful!"

"C'mon, you guys," Annelise says. "That's us!" She pulls the other girls toward the makeup mirror, but

I follow along more slowly, like I'm wearing too-big shoes, thinking about my family.

Just as I'm about to sit down in the last chair, another girl butts in front of me. She's even pushier than Annelise! The girl sits down and swivels toward the mirror, even though it's obvious she's already had a makeover. Her eyelids sparkle with glittery shadow, and her hairdo has purple highlights, just like mine did for Annelise's party.

"Excuse me," I say to the girl. "I'm Victoria Torres. They just called my name, and that's my chair."

The girl swivels back to face me. "*I'm* Erika Holmes," she sasses. "My hairdo needs a redo. You'll have to wait." She swivels away from me and starts primping in the mirror.

My mouth drops open. "But it's my birthday, and these are my friends!" I tell her, pointing to the girls.

Erika looks at my reflection in the mirror and shrugs. "Not my problem."

Bea jumps into the conversation. "It's *our* turn!"

Erika makes a face at Bea. "Don't have a freak-out. This isn't kindergarten."

Annelise and the other girls look down the row of chairs. "OMG," I hear Annelise say as Bea argues with Erika. "I remember that girl from summer camp. She's even meaner than I am!"

One of the staff notices the commotion and comes over. "What's the trouble here?" she asks.

"*That* girl took Vicka's chair!" Bea snarls.

Erika smiles sweetly at the woman. "I don't see what the big deal is. I just need a few more bobby pins."

"Certainly," the woman says to Erika. She looks at me. "We're running a little behind today with all the excitement over Queen Callie's visit, so could you *please* be patient? I'll get to you shortly."

She motions for me to move off to the side.

Erika smirks at my reflection in the mirror as I back away. I lean against the check-in counter, feeling very *un*spa-tacular.

Chapter 14

A Spa-tacular Surprise

"Are you waiting for a makeover?" I hear someone say. Looking across the check-in counter, I see a young woman smiling at me.

I nod. "It's my birthday party, but all the chairs are full."

"Well, happy birthday!" she says, stepping out from around the counter. She's pretty, with blue eyes and averagely brown hair, like mine. Babydoll tee. Faded jeans. Lace-up sneakers. "What's your name?"

"I'm Victoria," I say. "Vicka, for short. Do you work here? Could you do my makeover? My friends are already getting theirs done."

"Sorry, no," she says. "I'm here on *royal* business."

"Oh," I say, glancing out the store entrance at the Bling Mobile. "Are you helping Queen Callie?"

"Close," she says, smiling cheerfully. "I *am* Queen Callie."

I do a double take. "You're Queen Callie? But you look so *ordinary*!"

As soon as I say it, I clamp my mouth shut, wishing I could take it back.

But Queen Callie just laughs. "I'm a *casual* queen," she says. "I like being myself, and I'm happy you noticed."

"I thought queens wore fancy gowns and tiaras," I say.

"Sometimes I do," Queen Callie says. "But it's hard to haul books around in a big dress and heels! Could you help me for a minute? There are lots of girls here, and I'd love it if everyone went home with a new book to read. I've got tons in the Bling Mobile. I could use a hand carrying in a couple boxes."

"Okay!" I say.

I follow Queen Callie to the Bling Mobile. I tell her that Abuela met her at the library, and that Mom's book club is going to help her buy more books. "That's great!" Queen Callie says as we take two crates of books from the back of the cart. "I can always use more. The Bling Mobile will be empty again after the parade."

Queen Callie asks about my birthday as we carry the books inside. I've just started to tell her about my friends and our Space Odyssey mini makeovers when Bea rushes up to us. Her eyes sparkle with blue eyeshadow and tiny galaxies of stick-on stars shimmer on her cheeks.

"That awful girl, Erika, finally left," she tells me. "Come get your makeover!"

But suddenly putting on makeup doesn't feel as glamorous as helping Queen Callie. I turn to her. "This is my best friend, Bea." I explain. "Bea . . . this is Queen Callie!"

Bea's glittery eyes go wide. "Nice to meet you, Queen Callie!" she says, shaking hands with her.

"It's nice to meet you too, Bea! But please, you guys, call me *Callie*." She turns to me. "Thanks for helping with the books, Vicka! I can take it from here. Go have fun with your friends. Will you be staying for the parade?"

"*Staying* for it?" Annelise walks up to us with Jenny, Katie, and Grace. They all dazzle with glitter and stars. "We want to *be* in it." She makes a face at Callie's outfit. "Did I hear Bea say you're a queen? Where's your crown and sash?"

"In my daypack," Callie says. "I'll put them on in time for the parade."

Annelise crosses her arms. "It's Vicka's birthday, so she should be your Queen-for-a-Day. And since we're her best friends, she wants all of us ride on the Bling Mobile."

"I wish you could," Callie says. "But it's filled with books! And I'll be drawing names at random for prizes, including Queen-for-a-Day." She looks at me again. "Maybe I'll draw your name, Vicka! I hope so! Good luck!"

Lars hurries over to us. "Callie? A reporter from the Middleton newspaper is on his way. He wants to take photos of you with the girls, okay?"

"Sure!" Callie says. "I'll grab my bling!"

Callie goes behind to the check-in counter and pulls a tiara and sash from her bag. Meanwhile, my friends lead me to the makeup mirror and offer lots of help as I get glamorized.

Lars gathers everyone under a big GlamaRama! sign that hangs on one of the walls.

When the reporter arrives, Callie joins us for a photo shoot! Bea nudges me and says, "Look how pretty Callie looks in her sash and crown! *Now* she's a real glamour queen."

I have to agree with Bea. Callie is pretty, but I think she was glamorous before she put on her sash and crown. She doesn't need bling to shine.

"Say 'Cheese!'" the reporter says.

"Cheese!" we all shout, smiling for the camera.

Mom arrives and stands in the store's entrance with other parents, watching as we pose for the camera.

When the photo shoot is finished, the reporter talks with Callie while Lars and the other staff hand out books to all the girls.

Then Callie starts drawing names from the pink safari hat for prizes from the Bling Bin. Jenny and Grace both win prizes from our group!

"And now for the grand prize drawing," Lars says putting all the names back into the hat. "The winner will be crowned Queen-for-a-Day and ride in the mall parade!"

Callie stirs the names around and around inside the hat. I look at Mom. She crosses her fingers and smiles at me as Callie draws out a folded slip of paper.

I cross my fingers too, hoping she reads my name.

"And the winner is . . ." Callie says, unfolding the paper. "Erika Holmes!"

Erika squeals and hurries to Callie's side. Callie places a sparkly tiara on Erika's head.

No fair!

I look over at Mom. She uncrosses her fingers and shrugs her shoulders.

All my feelings of disappointment — missing my family party, missing out on a trip to the aquarium with Abuela, *not* being chosen Queen-for-a-Day boil up inside me. My eyes fill with hot tears. But I don't feel like stamping my feet and throwing a tantrum. There's only one thing I want to do right now, and I don't care if everyone in the world thinks it's babyish.

With tears spilling from my eyes, I zigzag past the girls that have mobbed around Erika, walk over to Mom, and let her give me a hug.

"I really wanted to be a queen for my birthday," I sob against her shoulder.

"You are, Vicka," Mom says. "You're my Queen of Hearts."

Erika and her friends bump past us, jabbering with excitement as they head out of the store to take pictures by the Bling Mobile.

My friends gather around me and Mom. Suddenly, I feel embarrassed to be crying like Lucas does when things don't go his way. I take off my glasses and wipe away my tears.

"Who wants to be a dumb old queen, anyway," Annelise says as I put on my glasses again. "I'd rather hang out with you guys."

I smile at Annelise.

"Me too!" Bea says.

"Me three!" Jenny adds.

Katie and Grace put their arms around my shoulders. "Group hug!" they shout.

We all huddle up. Mom snaps a picture of me and

my friends. "Hey, girls, I have a favor to ask." I break away from the hug fest to see Queen Callie walking up to us.

"What is it?" I ask.

"There's sure to be a crowd at the food court," Callie says. "I could use some *princesses* to help me hand out books."

Annelise budges past us. "Did you say princesses?"

Callie nods. "No tiaras, but I do have *these*."

Callie starts handing around GlamaRama! punch cards.

BLING OF THE MONTH CLUB!

Good for one item of your choice from

~ THE BLING BIN ~

each month of the coming year!

☐ ☐ ☐ ☐ ☐ ☐ ☐ ☐ ☐ ☐ ☐ ☐

Annelise snorts. "I'm already a member." Then she snatches a card from Callie. "But I'll take another. *Twice* the glam!"

Jenny thinks to ask Callie for an autograph, and she signs all the punch cards for us! Looking at her signature, I see she's written a special message for me.

Happy birthday, Vicka!
Shine like you mean it!

Love, Queen Callie

We gather behind the Bling Mobile as Erika and Callie hop in.

Callie toots the Bling Mobile's horn and then heads out, driving slowly around the mall. Mom waves goodbye as we princesses tag along, greeting shoppers and giving books to any kids who want them. As we loop back toward the GlamaRama!, I realize the float is behind me. I'm leading the parade! Not just around the mall, but straight into my twelfth year.

Callie was right. There is a big crowd at the food court, when we get there a few minutes later. Suddenly one section of the crowd starts shouting and jumping up and down. They hold a big, bright poster above their heads.

FELIZ CUMPLEAÑOS, Vicka! HAPPY BIRTHDAY!

It takes me a moment to realize the poster is for *me*! And the shouting people are *my family* — Dad, Sofia, Lucas, Abuela . . . even Aunt Selene and Uncle Julio and some of my other relatives are there! Mom joins them. Uncle Julio starts playing his guitar and everyone starts singing! The *whole crowd* joins in! Abuela steps forward. She waves her arms in the air, doing her goofy birthday dance.

¡Ay! I feel my cheeks burn with embarrassment under my makeup!

But then Bea runs over to Abuela and joins the dance! So does Jenny! Even Grace and Katie join in. Annelise rolls her eyes, but Jenny pulls her in, and a moment later, she's dancing too.

I look at my five friends, laughing and dancing with my family. No one looks silly. They all look spectacular!

Abuela holds her hands out to me. I take them and join the dance.

When the song is over, Abuela leads me to one of

the food court tables. There, sitting at the center, is an amazing triple-layer cake, decorated with a beautiful crown on top!

"For the birthday queen," Abuela says. "Just like I promised."

I give Abuela a big hug. Then I look at Mom and Dad. "But you said I had to choose . . . family party or friends party."

Mom glances at Dad. Then she shrugs. "I got outvoted. When you decided not to come to the party, the family decided to bring the party to *you*!"

"Hurry up, Vicka!" Lucas tells me. "Bite the cake! I want to show you what Abuela bought for me at the aquarium! A hermit crab! His name is Rocky. Wait until you see him!"

Abuela's eyes twinkle. She gives me a wink.

Mom shakes her head. "I got outvoted on that too."

Then my whole family starts chanting, like they always do. "*¡Mordida . . . mordida . . . mordida!*"

I look at Bea.

She smiles and says, "Go for it!"

I step up to the table and lean over my sparkly pink cake. As I take a bite, I feel a hand on the back of my head . . . two hands . . . three hands! My family and friends push my face into my beautiful cake!

Smoosh!

I come up laughing, my face and glasses covered with frosting. "How do I look?" I ask my friends.

Jenny laughs. "Delicious!"

"Nice makeover, sis," Sofia says with a teasing grin. "Happy birthday."

"Thanks!" I reply, taking off my frosting-covered glasses so I can see my sister. Then I see a boy peek past her shoulder. It's Joey Thimble!

"Happy birthday, Vicka," Joey says. "I hope you don't mind I crashed your party."

"Can I crash too?" I hear another boy say. Turning around, I see Drew walking up to me in his Boy Scout uniform. He glances back toward the candy booth. "I left Henry in charge."

Drew gives me the once-over, then leans in. "Um ... Vicka? You've got a little frosting on your face," he jokes.

I laugh. "Do I?"

Drew grins. Then he glances around at my family — laughing, taking pictures, slicing birthday cake. "I've been watching your family get ready to surprise you since before the parade." He looks at me again. "Now I know why you're so *sweet*. Happy birthday, Vicka!"

Fortunately, there's so much frosting on my face he can't see me blush!

"How about a photo with Queen Callie for the newspaper?" the reporter from the GlamaRama! asks.

Quickly, Bea cleans off my glasses with a napkin. I put them on again as Callie poses next to me. Creepy Erika watches from the Bling Mobile with her friends. They laugh and point at the frosting that's still on my cheeks and chin. But it doesn't matter. I feel too *above* average to care.

When the reporter is done taking photos, I say, "Now it's my turn to take a picture."

I pull out my fancy new phone. Striking a glamorous pose, I take the first selfie of my twelfth year.

Grace looks at the picture on the screen. "Seriously, Vicka," she says, "that's the best selfie *evah*!"

All my friends crowd in for a look at the picture I took of myself — big smile, glittery stars around my eyes, pink frosting covering my face! Best of all, my family and friends are right there, smiling in the background.

"*This* is my self-portrait," I say, showing the photo to everyone.

The picture doesn't just look like me, it *is* me — Victoria Torres. I'm a work of art!

About the Author

Julie Bowe lives in Mondovi, Wisconsin, where she writes popular books for children including *My Last Best Friend*, which won the Paterson Prize for Books for Young People and was a Barnes & Noble 2010

Summer Reading Program book. In addition to writing for kids, she loves visiting with them at schools, libraries, conferences, and book festivals throughout the year.

Always looking
for her way to shine!

BIRTHDAY
GLAMOUR!

FACE
THE
MUSIC

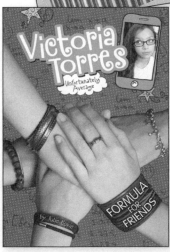

FORMULA
FOR
FRIENDS

POMPOM
PROBLEMS

Want More Victoria Torres?

Read the first chapter of...

Pompom Problems

My best friend, Bea, and I see the glittery blue and gold flier stuck to our locker as soon as we get to school on Monday morning.

> Hey, Muskrats!
> Here's Your Chance to Shine!
> Be a Middleton Middle School Football Cheerleader!
> Practices: After school
> Tryouts: Next Week
> Sign up in the Caf during lunch today!

"What's a Caf?" Bea asks, reading the flier. We've been sixth graders for only a few days, so we are still learning how to speak middle school.

"I think Caf is short for Cafeteria," I tell Bea.

Bea nods, thoughtfully. "Caf . . . cafeteria. Got it." She resnaps her sparkly barrettes in her dark, curly hair. "Not that it matters where the sign-up table is. The last thing we want to do is try out for cheerleading, right?"

"Wrong," I reply, tapping the bright flier with the tip of my pink-polished pointer finger. "It says here that cheerleading will make us shine!"

Bea blinks. "I already shine." She taps her sparkly barrettes. "Besides, we can barely do star jumps, Vicka, even though they're basically just jumping jacks. Not to mention cartwheels. And don't even get me started on the splits! Cheerleaders have to do stuff like that all the time. I should know. Jazmin has been cheerleading since she was our age."

Jazmin is Bea's older sister. She's in eighth grade, just like my brainy sister, Sofia. Unlike Sofia, Jazmin is a cheerleader. Everything about her shines, including her braces! She even went to cheerleading camp this summer.

"But we'll be poppies if we make the cheerleading squad," I reply.

Bea makes a face. "Poppies? Is that another middle school vocab word I need to learn?"

"Poppies is short for popular girls," I explain. "I just made it up. You know, like Annelise? Don't you want to be as popular as her?" Annelise has been the most popular girl in our class since kindergarten. She and her little brother always get the newest and coolest gadgets and toys. They have big, fancy parties too, because their parents are rich. For her ninth birthday party, Annelise's parents hired a magician. For her tenth, they rented a giant bouncy castle. Last year, for her eleventh, a limo picked us up and drove us to a teen concert in the city. We even got to meet the band backstage! Who knows what they'll do this year. Fly us all to London for lunch with the queen? Sometimes I wish my parents would spoil me like that.

"Annelise is a bully, not a poppy," Bea says. "Girls only hang out with her to stay on her good side."

I sigh. What Bea said is true. Annelise bullies everyone, even her so-called friends. I don't want to be a bully. But I do want to be a poppy!

"But, Bea," I reply, "popular girls really know how to shine. That's why they always wear cool sunglasses. To shield their eyes from the glare."

Bea makes another face.

I close my eyes, imagining myself standing under the field lights, cheering in front of the packed bleachers at a Middleton Muskrats football game! My family is there. Dad is wearing his lucky baseball cap and whistling through his fingers. Mom is waving the glittery Muskrat pennant she made from her scrapbooking supplies. Lucas is jumping around and waving the pennant he made out of duct tape and toilet paper tubes. And Sofia, hunched a few seats away, is adjusting her earbuds and pretending she doesn't know them. All while I shake two shiny blue and gold pompoms and yell my lungs out.

Kids from my class are there too — even some of

the boys like Henry, Sam, and Drew. Especially Drew. I've had a crush on his since this summer when he did a cannonball off the side of the Middleton Municipal Pool and totally drenched me with water. He cracked up when he saw me standing there, dripping. Then he splashed even more water at me!

At first I was angry, because I hadn't changed into my swimsuit yet. But then he bought a blue ice pop at the concession stand and shared it with me to say he was sorry. Blue is my favorite flavor! Everyone knows that boys are ice-pop hogs. They only share them if they like you.

Does Drew like me? I'm not sure, but I do like him. No one knows this, except for Bea.

When I open my eyes again, Bea is still making the face. "I don't care about being a poppy. All I care about is getting to class on time. C'mon, or we'll be late!"

"*Pleeeease*, Bea," I beg, as she drags me down the hallway. "I want to be a cheerleader more than anything, and I need to be a poppy. Try out for the squad with me!"

Bea stops and rolls her pretty eyes, which are even browner than mine. "Fine," she says. "I'll sign up with you, but not because I want to be a cheerleader or need to be popular. I'll try out because you're my BFF."

I give Bea a hug. "You won't regret it, Bea! Our world is about to change!"

I step back and do an awkward star jump. Fortunately, Bea ducks before I whack the barrettes out of her hair. Unfortunately, my hand smacks against a locker.

Thwunk!

"*¡Ay!*"

"Ouchies, Vicka!" Bea cries. "Are you okay?"

I nod, shaking away the pain in my wrist, then push my glasses back up on my nose. "I'm better than okay," I reply. "I am Victoria Torres . . . Cheerleader!"

Find out more about Victoria's
unfortunately-average life, plus
get cool downloads and more at
www.capstonekids.com

(Fortunately, it's all fun!)